MW00718316

SAM CRESCENT

EVERNIGHT PUBLISHING ®

www.evernightpublishing.com

Copyright© 2018

Sam Crescent

Editor: Karyn White

Cover Artist: Sour Cherry Designs

Jacket Design: Jay Aheer

ISBN: 978-1-77339-581-4

SAM CRESCENT

DEDICATION

I want to thank my readers and also Evernight Publishing for all of your support.

This is for all the alpha fans out there.

SAM CRESCENT

THE ALPHA'S VIRGIN POSSESSION

The Alpha Shifter Collection, 3

Sam Crescent

Copyright © 2014

Chapter One

Nick Long glanced down at his watch for the seventh time within the last ten minutes. He hated being kept waiting. All of his time earned him money, and the fact he'd been waiting for ten minutes meant he'd lost at least a million dollars. No one made him lose money. It pissed him off that this bastard thought he could be different. If it wasn't for the goods he particularly wanted, Nick would be long gone.

The only pleasure he got in his life was the knowledge of making money, more money than he'd ever need in a lifetime. Still, since being outlawed and forced to leave his pack and to never join another pack, Nick's life was about making money. There was no greater purpose in life than making money, especially when everything else had been taken from him. Keeping a firm hold on the case by his side, he waited for the sounds and smell of an approaching wolf. He was an alpha wolf, or he would be if he was allowed the right of his rank. Instead, he had it taken away from him, along with everything else.

He bore the mark of an outlawed wolf. Rubbing his chest, he tried not to think of the pain the silver mark had left in his chest. There were nights he jerked awake screaming at the memory of being held down, the flesh above his heart cut open and the silver poured inside to mark him as damaged. The silver still lay in his chest. Being a wolf stopped him from absorbing the silver or forcing it out. Everyone would know the collective had cast him out like a piece of scrap meat. The scar served as a reminder to him and to let others around him know he was dangerous.

Until he died every time he stared into the mirror he'd see the mark and know he wasn't anything but shameful.

Rubbing the back of his neck, he wondered about this night's purchase. He shouldn't be doing it, but his friend, Dean, promised him it was fine. Some wolf members sold the runts of their litters to anyone who would have them. Nick needed to keep it secret as this was the only way he would ever get a woman with wolf blood.

Finding out he could purchase a woman, an outcast from her pack, for the right money had given him hope to finally have something else to look forward to.

Another glance down at his watch and he was ready to leave. He wasn't going to be treated like an asshole just because he wanted a woman. Heading back to his car, he stopped at the sound of an approaching vehicle. Tensing, he turned toward the sound and saw the headlights coming nearer. The scent of wolf drifted toward him. Excitement took away all of his anger. This is what he'd been wanting ever since he'd stumbled onto the auction. By the end of the night he'd have a wolf female in his bed to do with as he pleased. No one would take her away or stop him from fucking her. He would possess every inch of her.

Love hadn't been part of his purchase. He was tired of holding back from fucking human women. Nick knew he needed a wolf to take the hard fuck he really wanted to give. None of the human women could take the length of his cock without feeling pain. Then there was the problem of them needing time to accommodate him. It was tiresome, and he'd grown tired of the light fuck. He craved a hard, rough fucking, and for a woman to pant and beg as he fed her his dick.

The car came to a stop several feet away from him. He watched the passenger side of the car open and an older man in his late fifties get out. Nick scented the air, inhaling the cruelty of the man. He tensed up in case this was a trap.

"You got the money?" he asked.

Names had been exchanged, and he knew it was Mark he was talking to. The other man was not an alpha, and Nick knew he could take him if things got dangerous.

"You got my prize?"

Mark snapped his fingers. The back door on the driver's side opened. A woman with long blonde hair stepped out of the back of the car. He sensed the evil within her as well. This couple was awful, what the fuck were they doing. Seconds later he saw the leash the woman was holding, which was attached to someone.

"Get your fat ass out of the car," the woman growled to someone in the back.

Inhaling the air, Nick smelled something wonderful and fresh like the roses in his garden. He'd never smelled anything quite so beautiful before in his life. Red hair caught his attention first as the woman he'd purchased climbed out of the car. He didn't see all of her until the woman rounded the car. The leash was tied around the girl's neck, and clearly it was tight from the red sores already developing. His anger once again started to build. What were these fuckers hoping to achieve by hurting her?

Why were they selling her?

The girl smelled like fear. Fear and pain wafted off her making him feel like a jerk. The whole act took on a whole new meaning, but he couldn't stop it. His need for her outweighed anything else.

"Here, this is the girl." Mark stepped forward, tugging her leash out of the blonde's hand.

"I hate having *it* around my place. Make sure he takes *it*," the blonde said, storming away.

"Come on, Clara," Mark said, forcing her to move.

"Why are you selling her?"

Clara, the redhead, was covered in large clothes that hid her entire body from view. Her head was downcast, but he saw the tears rolling down her cheeks. He couldn't begin to imagine the humiliation she would be feeling.

"She's too fat. Her presence is making us a laughingstock of the pack, but you wouldn't have a clue about that seeing as you've got no pack of your own."

Striking out, Nick grabbed the man around his neck, squeezing the life out of him. "I suggest you watch your language," he said.

In the background he heard the blonde screaming for him to release her husband. Ignoring her, Nick glared at the other man wanting to end his life. He was no longer an alpha, but no one was going to treat him with such disrespect without getting his anger directed at them.

"You're outlawed," Mark said, saying the words through gritted teeth.

Drawing him closer, Nick made sure he could be heard. "Exactly, so I don't give a fuck who I kill now. You try to fuck with me and I'll make sure you regret it." Removing the leash from the man's hand, he shoved him away, kicking the briefcase by his side toward the man as he did.

"Mark, baby, what's he done to you?" the blonde said, running to Mark's side. They were fucking vultures, and Nick hated them.

"Get the fuck out of my sight." Nick waited until the two were in the car and leaving before he turned his gaze to the woman at his side.

Clara—such a sweet name for a sweet woman—stared at him, terrified.

They were selling her because of her weight. If he was the alpha of their pack, he'd make sure her parents suffered a fate worse than death. Seeing as he was neither an alpha of a pack nor part of one, their ugliness had given him a woman.

Turning her head this way and that, he sensed her fear increasing.

"I'm not going to hurt you," he said, hoping his words would ease her. Taking her hand, he led her toward his car.

Crap. He had hoped for this night to run smoothly. From the way Clara was acting, he doubted she'd be ready to fuck when he got back home.

****

For many years Clara had heard the term "runt of the litter" when people talked about her. She hated it but pretended the words no longer affected her. Being told she was fat, ugly, and hated by all of the pack hadn't prepared her for the final humiliation she'd been dealt this night. The words hurt, but she'd grown used to them.

Sitting alone in her room reading one of her

favorite romances, she'd been pulled out of her fantasy by her mother. The leash, along with the clothes not to mention the complete destruction of her room, had been the last straw in the brutal pain.

The man who purchased her started up the car, taking her away from everything she knew. Her family and pack despised her, but at least she knew what they thought of her and nothing they said or did worried her. Apart from the bullying she'd been more than ready for whatever they wanted to dish out. The leash around her neck was wrapped around his wrist stopping her from moving.

Biting her lip she tried to force back the tears. Crying was an unnecessary weakness she couldn't afford. The silence in the car gave her little comfort. What would happen when they were alone in his home? She didn't know who he was or why he'd purchased her.

No matter how many diets she went on or the number of times she starved herself the weight wouldn't drop off. When she failed to lose any weight, the name calling would start back up. After the name calling started, she'd start eating again. The cycle would never end. Their harsh words and nastiness would send her back to food.

Scrubbing a hand over her face, she tried to get her nerves under control. Her hands were shaking like crazy.

They drove for the next hour without a word spoken. Clara was pleased by the lack of conversation. Trying to talk while being absolutely petrified was hard. Stringing a sentence together was impossible at the moment with her nerves.

Nick stopped the car in front of a large iron gate. He typed in a code she didn't see. The gate opened up, and he drove down. Glancing behind her she saw the gate close back up, trapping her inside with a man she did not know.

Looking across from the gate she saw the wall that had to be close to eight feet tall.

"I like my privacy," he said.

Turning back to face the front, she saw the large house was surrounded by a large array of fields, trees, and bushes. The car stopped, and the man turned to look at her. "I'm going to release you. If you make any attempt to run, move, or cause me problems, then I will have you locked up in a cage, do I make myself clear?" he asked.

"Yes."

He released the lead and climbed out. Staying in her seat, Clara waited for him to let her out. She wouldn't dare make a run for it. He opened the door, and she got out, waiting for him to give her more instructions. The thought of feeling any more pain kept her from running. She'd suffered enough pain to last her a lifetime, and she wasn't into any kind of weird fetish of feeling pain.

"Follow me." He headed inside the house. No one was in sight, and from the look and smell of the place, no other pack member was here. "Dean, I'm back," he said, shouting out.

Nick removed his jacket then reached out.

Unable to stop herself, Clara flinched away from his touch.

"I'm not going to hurt you."

Nodding, she stayed still as he took the leash from around her neck. "Does it hurt?" he asked.

She shook her head. The pain would soon ease.

"You're not lying to me, are you?"

"No, the pain will go away in no time." She glanced up at him.

"Is this the woman you just bought?"

A large man was walking downstairs. He wore a white shirt and a pair of scruffy jeans.

"Yeah." Nick wrapped his fingers around her neck, pulling her close.

"Well, you're back, and you're alive. Did anything happen I need to know about?" Dean said.

"No, nothing happened that he didn't bring on himself."

"What do you mean?" Dean asked, looking nervous.

"I took care of business. I'm not pack anymore, and any problems can come to my fucking door. I don't care what anyone says." Nick's voice was harsh, demanding, and she detected a hint of hurt.

"Shit, you're right, I'm sorry." Dean rubbed the back of his neck with a flush to his cheeks.

"Don't worry about it."

She watched Dean grab his jacket from the back of the door and was on the way out when he stopped as Nick started to talk.

"Tell the packs that if they want to fuck with me then fine, fuck with me, but warn them, I don't play by the fucking rules. They start, they'll end up dead."

"Nick…"

"No, I mean it, Dean. I'm done playing their games. They want to play, then I'll play them, but I'll do it my fucking way."

Dean looked sad, glancing at her before nodding his head.

"See you soon."

"You will."

The door opened then closed, leaving her alone with a man who'd just threatened at least two packs that she knew of.

"Now, we can have some real fun," he said,

keeping a grip on her neck and leading her toward the stairs.

Her nerves picked up, and she started to fight him.

"Please, let me go. I've done nothing wrong. I've always been good."

Nick caught her around the waist, holding her arms by her sides.

"Stop!" He yelled the word, and she had no choice but to stop.

They were the only two people in the room, but she knew deep in her core he was the alpha. She couldn't argue with him even if she wanted to. He was the man who made the rules.

"You're not going anywhere, so stop fucking testing me. No one wants you but me. You've got no one but me, and it's time for you to start realizing it." He shouted the words in her face, and she couldn't stop the tears from filling her eyes and then falling down her cheeks. Every word he spoke was the truth.

She was at his mercy, and there was no way out of it.

Chapter Two

Nick felt the fight go right out of her. Loosening his hold, he waited for her to submit. Her head bowed within seconds of her body relaxing. Releasing his tight grip, he tilted her head back to look at him.

Clara's scent and body didn't repel him at all. Buying a wolf online had been troublesome, and he had been worried about what she would look like. The only word to describe Clara was beautiful. Her family didn't see what a prize they possessed. Many wolf males, even alphas, would have taken her off their hands.

Their loss was his gain.

Tears fell down her cheeks, cutting him up at the sight. "Don't cry."

"I'm not allowed to feel now, either?" she asked.

She looked completely lost.

Staring into her eyes, he was struck by the glorious shade of green. Running his thumb across her smooth cheek, he moved toward her lips. She showed no sign of jerking away. Her lips were plump, heart-shaped. He couldn't wait to see how they felt pressed against his own.

"You're allowed to feel whatever you like, but know this, I will never hurt you."

"You just paid money for me. What am I supposed to think?"

Letting out a breath, he took hold of her arm and led her upstairs. Yes, he'd paid money for her, but he wasn't a complete animal.

She doesn't know that.

"Are you a virgin?" he asked, choosing not to think about her question or his own doubts about his purchase of a wolf.

"That's none of your business."

He stopped, turning to look at her. She may be scared, but she still had a mouth on her. There was no getting away from her question. "Like you so aptly put it, I bought you. For all you know I've bought you for sex. To use you for my pleasure."

Her cheeks were heating with every word he spoke. Nick also scented her desire. Clara was turned on by his words. *Interesting.* He'd never thought a female could be turned on by the prospect of being bought for money and then used for sex.

She stayed silent for several seconds.

"Are you going to use me?"

"Are you a virgin?" He counteracted her question with one of his own. She bit her lip, refusing to answer.

Staring down her body, Nick wished for the layers of clothing to be removed so he could admire her body.

"I didn't buy you for your thrilling conversation," he said, finally hoping to shock her into confessing the truth. "I bought you because I was getting tired of fucking human women. They can't take the pounding I wish to give. Yes, I bought you for sex. I bought you for the pleasure you'll give my cock."

Her cheeks were a lovely strawberry color. Nick wondered how far he could talk to get the combination of her embarrassment and the scent of arousal.

"You're outlawed."

"Yes."

"What for?"

Nick smiled. Leaning against the wall, he opened the door. "Go inside, and I'll tell you everything you want to know."

She looked inside the room. Her hand went to her chest, covering her breasts. Fuck, his cock thickened looking forward to seeing those plump mounds.

"Come on, Clara. Come inside, and I'll tell you everything you want to know."

"If I don't want to?" she asked, not taking a step closer.

"Then you can go into the bedroom next door, but I won't tell you a single thing."

How far did her curiosity go? Nick waited, loving the challenge she represented. She took a step toward the room then pulled away.

"No, I wish for my own room."

He was annoyed but also happy. She offered him a challenge, and he looked forward to breaking down her resolve to get what he wanted.

"Are you sure?" he asked, trying to tempt her. Unbuttoning his shirt, he left it to lie open for her to be able to see him.

Her gaze wandered down the length of him before jerking back up to his face.

She smelled fucking amazing. He couldn't wait to bury his head between her breasts and then her thighs, to taste every single inch of her soft body. His excitement was hard to contain at the prospect of the future.

"Yes, I'm sure. I'd like my own room."

"You're not interested in finding out why I'm outlawed?"

"I'm interested, but I'm also not stupid." Her fingers were locked together in front of her. Trying to ward him off? He wondered. "You'll end up doing more than talking in there." She nodded into his room.

"You're right." He shrugged. "We'll see how long this lasts." Brushing past her, the smell of her arousal increased. Hiding his smile, he opened the door to her bedroom. He'd gotten it ready over a week ago when he'd been in negotiation for his woman.

Clara had no choice but to brush past his body in

order to get past him.

It took every ounce of strength not to touch her or draw her closer to him. The clothes she wore looked filthy, not to mention the red marks around her neck. He hated the sign of the pain she must have clearly gone through.

The room was decorated in a lovely lilac color with matching sheets for the double bed he purchased. The walk-in wardrobe was empty, but he'd go onto stocking up on all the clothes she would need.

There was a vanity table in the corner, and the doors opened up onto a veranda that overlooked the entire grounds. The property had been expensive when he bought it for the size of the land. Being an outlawed wolf didn't stop him from needing to run.

"You're wealthy, or is all of this family money?" she asked, folding her arms.

Glancing at her breasts, Nick let out a growl. She gasped, dropping her hands and taking a step back.

"You're a wolf?"

"Of course I'm a wolf. I'm an outlawed wolf, but what's more, I was an alpha until they kicked me out of my position." He took a step closer, then another until they were standing close to each other.

She held her hands up. "I've heard of humans who cannot turn being outlawed, which is why I didn't know if you were a wolf or not." Clara tried to ward him off, but he wasn't having any of it.

Reaching up, he sank his fingers into her thick red hair. His cock hardened painfully against the zipper of his trousers. Clara's submission was going to be a challenge he looked forward to conquering. She'd be his reward at the end of the long fight.

****

Clara waited for him to say more. She didn't

know why she asked him about being a wolf. Of course he was a wolf. The smell along with the depth of his voice told her he was an alpha. She didn't know why there was no pack, and there certainly were no signs of a pack. Dean hadn't been part of the pack either.

"Are you a virgin?" he asked.

Glancing down at the floor, Clara stayed quiet. Clara didn't know why she didn't tell him the truth. For once, she wanted to keep a little part of herself to herself. She wasn't going to tell him the truth yet. Being a virgin within a pack wasn't something to boast about. During the full moon of a female's eighteenth birthday, many women lost their innocence. The men would surround them, take what they wanted, and come morning they'd be full women in every sense of the word.

No man had gone near her on her eighteenth or nineteenth birthday. When all the pack were fucking, she'd scampered away to be alone and mourn what she could never have. Some of the pack females enjoyed teasing her and taunting her lack of love life. Shaking her head to clear the horrid images from her mind, she looked up at him.

"You're not going to tell me?" he asked.

"No, why should I?"

Stop fighting, you idiot. He can do anything he wants with you.

He intrigued her. Nick was a mystery. She'd never heard about him before. Most outlaws were discussed in great detail amongst packs, but she couldn't fit his circumstances with the name of any outlawed wolves.

"We're going to play this game, I see."

"It's not a game. I don't have to tell you anything." She was terrified and couldn't stop the words from spilling out of her mouth. The grip in her hair tightened pulling her head back, exposing her neck. *Stop goading him.*

"No. I'm an expert in getting what I want, Clara. I'll have you begging for me to fuck you by the next full moon."

"How dare—"

She didn't get to finish her statement when his lips smashed down on hers, cutting off any angry protest she wanted to start with him. Outraged by the kiss, she opened her mouth, getting ready to push him away with her fists, and he took advantage, plundering her mouth with his tongue.

Pressing her palms to his chest, Clara had every intention of pushing him away when his free hand curved around her ass. She'd never been touched in such a passionate way before. There was no control over her responses. Her nipples budded against her shirt as her pussy melted. The wetness seeped into her panties. She was mortified at her response to him. The man who bought her shouldn't be getting this kind of response from her. In that moment she hated herself and her body for being so weak.

He held her tightly. She felt the evidence of his happiness pressing against her stomach. His tongue stroked her lips before sliding inside, meeting with his own.

She had every intention of pushing him away from her. With his hands and tongue exploring her body, she couldn't bring herself to push him away. Her body felt odd, different with his touch.

Nick pulled away first, smiling. "See, I can smell how wet your pussy is, baby. You want me, and I'm going to find out soon if you're a virgin. Don't worry, I can wait." He put his hands between her thighs, cupping the evidence of her need.

Swatting his hand away, she glared, hoping he'd stop tormenting her. "You're a hateful man."

"No, I'm not. I'm a man who knows what he wants and goes after it without thought." He claimed her lips once again, showing her who was boss. "Don't think to hide or fight me. You'll lose."

He stormed out of the room in the next breath.

Lips tingling, breasts tight, and a heat between her legs that made her feel like she was burning alive, she turned away from the door. No, she refused to let the man who bought her like she was some kind of possession affect her. She wrapped her arms around her body, trying to hold onto some kind of sanity.

You like him.

She shook her head. There was no way she could like him. He was a monster who'd bought her. She opened two doors discovering the en-suite bathroom. Entering the room, she turned on the shower before removing her clothes. Being bought didn't mean she couldn't be clean.

Standing under the hot water, she ran a hand down her naked body feeling his touch once again.

Her nipples were rock hard even with the warm water. Nick Long, he was going to get under her skin and infuriate her. He was used to getting what he wanted while she was used to being ignored. Their circumstances were completely the opposite and scared her.

The unknown always scared her. The men and women in the pack took great satisfaction in ignoring her apart from ridiculing and mocking her. Wiping a hand over her face, she let out a breath. Her life had changed in a blink of an eye.

After she finished washing, she wrapped the large white towel around her body then headed toward the mirror. She wiped away the steam and checked out the red sores around her neck. They would disappear soon, but they irritated her.

She ran her fingers over the red line, gritting her teeth.

You're away. You're free.

Clara wasn't free. She was at the mercy of a man she didn't know. Was Nick hiding some horrid secret? Why was he outlawed?

None of the answers she wanted would come to her through her reflection. Letting out a frustrated growl, she left the bedroom.

Coming up short, she saw an oversized shirt resting on the bed. The shirt hadn't been there when she left the room. She checked the door before standing before the bed. Clara couldn't help but be touched. He'd left her a shirt to wear.

Drying her body, she quickly put the large shirt over her head, smelling him instantly. She was shocked the fabric fit over her large body. Smiling, she climbed into bed and settled down. Maybe he wasn't so awful after all.

Chapter Three

Nick left the shirt, but he didn't leave without looking at her lush body first. He found her naked in the shower with eyes closed looking up at the shower jet. Her body was so full and round, she made him ache with need to possess her. She'd take the fucking he so wanted to give her.

He left the bathroom before she scented him close by. The smell from the bath soaps along with the noise of the shower would stop her from hearing him. Nick closed all the doors so she wouldn't know he'd been in apart from the nightshirt.

Sitting down on the edge of his bed, he ran a hand down his face. His cock was rock hard and showed no signs of diminishing even though he wanted it to. There was no female close enough apart from Clara to fuck.

The game was set. She would fight him at every turn, but he felt the need inside her body. In no time at all she'd be begging him for more, and he intended to give her everything.

Removing his clothes, he didn't bother with a shower. He changed into a robe then left his room to check through the whole house. No one ever bothered him out here. His security was tight, the electrical systems top of the range.

Going into his security room he checked the cameras and made sure the codes were all in place before locking the front door at the press of a button.

He tried not to think about the kiss or the feel of her lush body pressed against his own. Blocking all the thoughts from his mind, he headed back upstairs, pausing outside of her room. There was no sound coming from behind the door. He half expected her to come out, cursing and shouting at his audacity to enter the room.

Turning the knob, he opened the door to find her curled up in the center of the bed. He entered the room, closing the door behind him. She didn't make any move. From the sound of her breathing she was in a deep sleep.

Leaning down, he stroked her cheek, hearing her sigh and roll over. Unable to resist holding her, he climbed in beside her, lifting up the cover. She didn't wake up. Clara must be exhausted not to wake up at the slightest movement.

If anyone tried to get into bed with him, he'd be up like a shot. Years of being an alpha had cemented his own protection.

He eased down then touched her arm. Again, she didn't wake at all. Frowning, he hated her lack of response.

Why? You could come here every night, and she wouldn't wake up to push you away.

Smiling at the sudden fun he could have, Nick wrapped his arms around her. She muttered something but curled up against him. Her hand rested underneath her chin. Staring down into her lovely face, he stroked the length of her red hair. The color looked like fire against the lilac pillow. He wondered what it would look like spread across his lap as she took his cock deep into her mouth.

The kiss they shared had been hot, fiery, and set his pulse ablaze with the feel of her against him. When she gave into him, their passion would be epic. There was no other word he could think of to describe their few precious minutes together. Pushing the blanket down, he saw she wore the shirt he gave. So, she would take gifts from him, providing he left them for her and gave her little choice but to accept them. The shirt he'd given her was one he wore late at night when he worked at home. It looked good on her.

From the size, he saw he was bigger than she was in a lot of ways. Running his fingers down her arm, he heard her sigh again. Her response to his kiss had to be a sure sign she was a virgin. There was no way a woman used to the attention would feel that way.

Buying a woman online had left a bitter taste in his mouth. Many times he looked at the price of a pack female wondering how many packs had given up wolves for money. When he'd controlled a pack, he had never put any of his pack members up for auction. Each person was to be cared for, loved. Selling them to some stranger would have incurred his wrath, and he'd have taken care of them. It had been well over ten years since he was in control of a pack, so things must have changed since he was last in charge.

Pushing the nasty thoughts out of his mind, he thought only about how wonderful Clara felt against him.

When she lifted a leg to rest near his cock, he almost lost control. The full moon was far off, but he didn't need the full moon to turn into his wolf form. He stared at the harsh red mark around her neck, thinking about the silver curse in his flesh. She had no right to be cast out, but he knew it was because of her weight.

Plenty of pack females were thin, slender, anorexic looking because of their fast metabolism. Some packs looked down on a woman with curves. He was not one of them. In fact, if he'd not been outlawed and had still been an alpha of a pack, he'd have taken a fancy to Clara regardless.

Her curves, her smell, drove him insane. From the moment she climbed out of the car, he'd been intrigued by her.

Kissing her forehead, he saw how vulnerable she was. Anyone could have hurt her in the old pack. He was never going to send her back home.

For Clara, her future would be filled by him, and he'd give her everything her heart desired.

Relaxing beside her, Nick closed his eyes waiting for sleep to claim him. He wrapped his arms around his new possession, happy and settled for the first time in his life.

If his parents could see him now, they'd be so happy for him. Clara was a fine female to call his own.

****

Waking up, Clara groaned against the reality of her situation. The sudden smell of Nick had her jerking awake, rubbing at her eyes. Glancing around the room, she expected to find him lurking, ready to pounce at any time. Going to her knees, she looked left and right then down at her body.

The smell had to have come from the shirt she was wearing. There was no sign of the man in the bedroom she slept in. Climbing off the bed, she looked around, finding no more clothes. Her own were filthy, and she wasn't wearing them.

Heading to the bathroom, she sorted through her morning routine of going to the toilet, washing her hands, then brushing her teeth to combing through her hair. She left the length to fall around her shoulders. Clara usually bound the length up to keep it out of her way.

Blowing out a breath, she grabbed a robe and walked downstairs. The sun was shining brightly through the kitchen. The double doors were wide open. She heard Nick arguing with someone. Stepping closer, she found him on the phone, yelling and pacing the patio.

Looking past his shoulders, she saw a table laden with food and drink. Her stomach growled. He jerked at the noise, staring right at her.

"I've got to go. Be ready for my call within the hour or it's your fucking job." He growled the last word into the phone then hung up.

"I'm sorry. I didn't mean to interrupt."

"Come outside. Breakfast is served."

Checking to make sure the robe was closed, she walked outside. The heat hit her, wishing she left the robe and had clothes in place of it.

"No one can see us. Take the robe off. You're going to sweat and start to stink badly," he said, taking a seat.

She watched him lift a large glass to his lips. How did he make drinking look so erotic? Fidgeting with the belt, she glanced at him seeing the smile on his lips. He was teasing her, testing her. She took the seat opposite him, and when he couldn't see her legs, she removed the robe.

His lips twitched, clearly happy with her.

"I may not be able to see your thighs, but I've got a clear view of those nipples, baby. You're turned on or cold, I wonder?"

"It's a little chilly," she said, hating him.

"I imagine you are." He sipped some more juice smiling at her.

Linking her fingers together, she stared at him, waiting.

"Eat, Clara. This food is yours as much as it is mine."

Gazing over the table she was shocked by how much was available. There were two piles of pancakes, breakfast cereal in many varieties, toast, butter, jam, and fruit.

"Erm, I can't eat everything."

"I don't expect you to. I want to see what you eat so I know for next time," he said. His elbow leaned on the handle on the chair, and he was leaning his head on his hand.

"You prepared this? Don't you have a housekeeper or something?" She reached for the cereal, milk, and a bowl.

"No, I've got a cleaning lady to come in twice a week. I can't be done with having someone around for so long. I hate the invasion in my life." He poured some more juice into a glass.

"Do you have to leave the house?" she asked.

"No. My business can be done from anywhere."

Great, she wouldn't be alone.

"Don't you want any sugar?" he asked, pointing to her cereal.

"No. I don't like sugar on my cereal." She wasn't lying either. Sugar made cereal too sweet for her.

He handed her a drink of juice before sitting back. She felt his gaze on her at all times. Clara tried to ignore him, chewing and staring off to her left to look around the garden.

"How did you sleep?" he asked.

Glancing back toward him, she saw he was smiling once again. "Fine." Did she miss something? His smile seemed to mean something. "Did you?" Her manners were never going to be destroyed even if she did hate him.

Why did she hate him? He'd not done anything to her. All he'd done was take her out of a bad situation. Her family hated her. The pack had been awful to her at every opportunity. None of them liked her in their company. Her life's meaning had been about avoiding them all at every opportunity.

"What are you thinking about?" he asked.

"What? Why do you want to know?" She lost her appetite and pushed the bowl of cereal away.

"You've gone sad, withdrawn even. I want to know what has made you feel that way."

He leaned forward, staring into her eyes. She hated how he seemed to see everything.

"Nothing."

"You're lying. I don't like liars, Clara. Never lie to me."

Licking her lips, she clasped her hands together, trying to focus on something other than him. "I was thinking about my family and my pack."

She dropped her head, not wanting him to see too much.

"Do you miss them?"

"No." She looked back up at him, knowing he deserved to see her gaze.

"Then why are thinking about them and feeling sad as you do?"

His questions were reasonable, but they felt to invasive to her. Hiding the truth away from him wouldn't do any good. Nick was a rich man. He got what he wanted by being ruthless.

"I was thinking about how happy they must have been to get me out of their pack." She smiled. "I wasn't a good advertisement for pack life at all. None of the men wanted anything to do with me, and the women stayed away from me, afraid my repellent would spread."

Clara didn't even realize until now how much their actions had hurt her.

Wiping away the tears that had caught her by surprise, she cursed her wayward emotions. If her mother was close by, she'd be getting a beating before the end of the day.

"They're gone, and they're never coming back," Nick said. "Besides, you should be worried about my attention. I promise you, Clara, when I pop your cherry you're not getting a moment's rest from me."

Chapter Four

"How do you know I'm a virgin?" Clara asked. Her eyes were wide, and Nick smiled. She truly was the most adorable female he'd ever known. She didn't know her own power, which was mightily refreshing. It was sweet yet unsettling. The pack she'd been part of was awful. The pain in her eyes let him know how badly she'd been treated. Each pack behaved differently, but from what he heard this morning, Clara's pack was an open group.

At the full moon, the pack mated with one another, fucking until the sun came up. He had heard they were in human form rather than wolf form. Dean was a vessel of knowledge when it came to pack traditions. Females at their proper mating age of eighteen were allowed to mingle with the pack for men to scent them. Clara on her mating day had been left alone. Not one male in the pack had anything to do with her.

Looking beyond her shoulder, he couldn't stop the anger at their treatment of her. They were fucking awful, and if he ever got chance to cause them pain, he would do it.

"I've got my way of knowing everything, baby."

"Then why did you ask me last night if you knew the answer?"

"I didn't know the answer last night. I bought a female wolf, not all the details." He shrugged. Their conversation was the most thrilling company he'd experienced in years. Dean was okay to talk with, but human females didn't hold a patch on Clara. Her face alone was fascinating to watch. All of her emotions were on display for him to read. For a wolf female she was very naive. No one had taught her the value of keeping her emotions in check. It wasn't a bother. He'd teach her everything she needed to know and more.

Her nipples were getting harder. The shirt he'd given her looked good against her curves. She pushed some of her hair out of the way as the slight breeze flung it against her face.

Nick sipped at more of his juice thinking about last night. He'd woken this morning to find her still deep in sleep, her body wrapped around his. He had taken great pains to leave her side without waking her up. When he'd stood over her, the blanket had revealed everything. The shirt she wore had ridden up to show most of her body. Her tits were still a mystery to him, but everything else was not.

The red of her hair was the same down below. She also didn't wax, which he loved. He looked forward to sliding the lips of her sex open to reveal her creamy cunt. There was nothing more pleasurable than tasting a woman's cum while listening to her screams of release.

"What did it say? Fat wolf ready for the taking, no man entered before."

Her anger annoyed him but not as much as her name calling.

"Not at all. You see yourself as fat."

She didn't keep her gaze on him. Her cereal was half eaten.

"Are you done with your food?" he asked.

"Yes," she said, snapping at him.

"Good, we can get straight into your punishment." He stood up, rounding the table and holding out his hand for her to take.

"What? Punishment for what? I've done nothing wrong beside argue with you. I'm not here because I want to be." She kept a firm grip on the handles of her chair.

"I've got few rules, Clara. You've broken one of

my rules, and I will not have it in my house. I've got a fitting punishment for you. Stand up now, or I will add more to your punishment." He waited for her to take his hand. Clara didn't. Her green eyes set him ablaze with the contemptuous look she sent his way. Didn't she have the first clue that everything she did was only turning him on? He was fucking rock hard, ready to fuck her at a moment's notice.

"You can't do this. It's unfair and wrong," she said, remaining in her seat.

"We can go inside the house to deal with your punishment, or we can deal with it outside. I've got an order of your clothes coming, and I will make sure our guests witness your punishment."

"You brute. Are you some kind of Dominant?" she asked.

"So you know what those are?"

Her cheeks flamed, but she didn't answer.

"No, I'm not a Dominant. I've got no playroom or equipment to punish you with. I don't own floggers. What I've got is my hand, some fancy dildos, and some rope. I don't need anything else to get my pleasure." Her gaze returned to his in shock. "What's it going to be, Clara? Punishment in privacy or for others to see?"

Slowly, she gave him her hand. Her fingers were shaking. Drawing her to her feet, he admired her body, the length of legs she tried to hide.

"You did that on purpose," she said, trying to bend down to cover her legs.

"You'll learn to give me everything I want and not try to hide yourself. Your punishment remains." He took her hand and led her back into the house. Nick stopped, thinking about the best place for her to have her punishment. The only room, besides the bedroom, that would do was the sitting room. The curtains were open, and glancing at the clock as he passed her saw their company didn't come for another two hours at least. They were free to do what they wanted until then.

"We're not going upstairs? What if someone comes?" she asked, pulling on his hand.

"You should have thought about that before you broke one of my rules."

She stamped her foot. "I didn't know your rules. This is wrong, Nick."

He liked the sound of his name coming from her lips too much.

"Then today you'll learn at least one of them." He wasn't going to hurt her, but he'd have her over his knee and feeling her against him.

Sitting down in the center of the sofa, he tapped his knee. "Over you go."

****

"You're being a complete and utter bastard," Clara said, fuming at his happiness. Her pussy was melting as well. She was so ashamed to be turned on over a punishment. One moment she wasn't getting any kind of attention, and now she got nothing but attention. It was driving her insane.

"I've been called worse, baby." He leaned back, showing off his knees. His thighs looked big enough to take her weight. No one had ever tried to get her to rest on them before. "Over you go. The longer you take risks someone seeing you."

Glaring at him, she stepped closer and moved over his knees. His hand banded around her waist, helping her in place. Her stomach rested in the gap between his legs with her breasts pressed to his thigh. Both of his hands moved her to how he wanted her. She was surprised he didn't make any noise when he put her into position. Her weight had no effect on him.

"There. That wasn't so hard was it?" he asked.

"What is my punishment?"

"You'll have to wait and see."

Lying across his legs, she held onto the fabric of his trousers waiting for him to give her a punishment.

One of his hands held onto her waist. She didn't know where his other hand was. He started to lift up the night shirt she wore. Clara waited and then suddenly realized she had no underwear on.

"Stop," she said.

"Well, Clara, I have to say I'm surprised at you. I thought you'd at least wear some kind of panties." The smile in his voice was hard not to detect.

"Are you laughing at me?"

"Not at all. It's nice to see you're a natural redhead."

"Oh God," she said, burying her head against his leg wishing he'd get her embarrassment over with. She'd suffered enough. He didn't have to prolong her misery with his words.

His hand lay on her ass, not moving.

"Your ass is fucking beautiful," he said, caressing the cheek.

She felt like she was going to burn alive at his touch. The room was light, and he'd be able to see every lump and bump within her flesh. Did she have cellulite on her ass? She didn't know. Looking at her ass in the mirror hadn't been part of her activities.

Down his touch went, curving over her ass then down her thighs.

"Your body is beautiful, Clara."

Not saying anything, she waited for him to be done with her.

"Punish me already," she said.

"No, I'm going to take my time."

He caressed her ass. Her response to his touch annoyed her. Nick shouldn't be inspiring a response from her.

"Do you want your punishment to be less severe?" he asked. His voice sounded strained to her.

"In what way?" She turned to look at the back of the sofa. Staring into his eyes was not a possibility at the moment. What if he was laughing at her?

"Nah, you see that would spoil our fun if I tell you want I want, Clara."

"Then you want me to agree without knowing what I have to do to stop my punishment being painful?"

How her life had changed in the matter of twenty-four hours. If she was living with her parents she'd be cleaning their house as they sat around doing nothing. She was nothing but a slave to her family.

"You've got to take a chance in life. Do you want to continue with a harsh punishment or take a chance and get one lighter?"

Resting her head on his thigh, she thought through what he was saying. Would it be so hard to take a chance with him? She didn't know the answer to her own questions. Nick confused her. What pain could be worse?

"Yes."

"Are you sure?"

No, she wasn't sure about anything anymore.

"Yes," she said, letting out a sigh.

His fingers caressed her ass. Suddenly, he lifted her up and stood. He spun her to face him.

Licking her dry lips, she stared up into his eyes. They were a dark amber as he looked down at her.

"I want you to take your nightshirt off for me."

"What? I'm not wearing anything else."

He sat down, resting his arms wide.

Glancing down at his lap she saw the ridge of his cock pressing against his trousers. Fucking hell, he was huge! The outline made her swallow past the lump in her throat.

"Get naked and I'll be happy to lighten your punishment."

"I'll be naked."

"That's the point. You'll be naked, and I'll finally get to see what I paid for."

His words thrilled her.

"This is far worse," she said, folding her arms over her chest.

"Is it? We're wolves, Clara. It's worse being confined in these fucking clothes than it is being naked." He pinched at the clothing, the disgust visible on his face.

"If you hate clothes so much why don't you take them off?" she asked.

"I would, but I figured if you came down to breakfast to see me naked you'd run at the first opportunity. I love a good run any other time. Breakfast and a run don't work for me at all."

He was right. If she'd seen him naked then she would have been nervous. Her family was happy being naked around each other, but she'd been banned from being naked. She was ordered to be covered at all times.

Clothes had become another layer of protection to her. She stood out in the pack as she was the only one wearing clothes during a meeting.

"Why do you want to see me naked?" she asked.

Nick stood, startling her at the speed with which he moved. Tensing, she watched him tear his shirt off then push his trousers off. He sat down, gripping his length and letting out a sigh. "Now, that's much better. It's natural for us to be like this, Clara. No more hiding, and embrace who you are."

He fisted his shaft looking at his arousal and then at her. "This, this is for you. This is what you do to me."

Fingering the shirt, Clara felt the need to claw out of the clothing. The first time she'd been ordered to wear clothes her whole skin had itched. Most of the women after they came of age, stayed naked. She had been forced to wear clothing.

Break free.

Could she really break free of all she'd known?

Chapter Five

The raw emotions playing across her face were tearing Nick apart. He wished he'd killed her parents the night before instead of letting them live. Their life was going to be too nice to them. They had used their daughter to see to that.

Fisting his cock, he settled all of his attention onto Clara. She needed him right now, not her parents. They had hurt her in ways he didn't understand. Nick knew he'd treat her like a queen.

He wouldn't tell her to stop. Nick wanted to see her naked, and he intended to. Not only did he want to see her naked, he also wanted her to be more relaxed around the house. He was used to wearing clothes and didn't need to be naked. From the information he'd gotten, Clara hadn't gotten the same satisfaction of running wild and naked during her turning. Her parents really deserved to suffer for what they had done to her.

Watching her gave him immense pleasure alone.

"Can't I go back and have a hard punishment?"

"No." *No backing down.* It would be so easy for him to give into her and leave her punishment be. "Being naked is not a hardship."

"Speak for yourself."

"I can wait all day. We've got guests coming," he said, reminding her.

She growled at him, stamping her foot.

"Cute," he said, smiling.

"Fine, let's get this over with." She lifted the shirt off her body, revealing her creamy flesh to his gaze. Her hips were wide, her stomach nicely rounded. Up his gaze went to stare at her full tits. They were perfect with large rounded red nipples. Her hands rested on her hips. "Well, what do you want me to do now?"

"Sit on the coffee table," he said.

He had to control himself so he didn't pull her onto his lap and pound inside her tight pussy.

She glanced behind her then lowered her ass to the wooden coffee table. He always knew it would come in handy when he bought it.

"Lean back on your hands."

Going to his knees before her, he gripped her knees, opening her thighs. Her arousal surrounded the room. The fragrance was heady, intoxicating, and sent the need to fuck coursing through him. She'd been left alone for far too long. Her mating need would be right around the corner, and he'd be the one to claim her.

Clara fought him to keep her thighs closed. He held her steady, refusing to let her close up on him.

"What are you going to do?" she asked.

"You're going to trust me to give you more pleasure than you could ever imagine."

She was panting for breath.

Her body remained tense even as he opened her thighs and drew her to the edge of the wooden coffee table.

Keeping his gaze on her he glided his hands up her thighs feeling the muscles quiver beneath his touch.

"Nick," she said, biting her lip.

"Don't worry about a thing, baby. I'm here, and I'm not going to do anything to hurt you."

She nodded but didn't change at all as he held her. Gazing down her body he settled his attention on the flush lips of her pussy. The dusting of red hair turned him on. Moving his fingers up he slid the lips of her sex wide open to reveal the nub of her clit.

His mouth watered as the smell of her cum drove him closer.

"What are you doing?" she asked.

"I'm going to taste you. When I'm done you're going to feel the sting of pleasure."

His cock was going to cause him more pain than he'd ever cause her. Leaning closer, he focused on her slit. Sliding his tongue across her clit, he moaned at the first explosion of taste from her. She was musky and sweet at the same time. Keeping her lips open, he slid down to tongue her entrance. Her virgin barrier prevented him from going further inside. He was tempted to dispense of her innocence with his fingers rather than wait to bury inside her with his cock.

The thought of claiming her and pumping his cum into her womb stopped him from getting rid of that pesky barrier.

Gliding up, he circled her clit. She collapsed back. The coffee table was big enough for her to lie back completely. Clara was a lot smaller than he realized. She'd take his cock, and he couldn't wait.

He gripped his cock, fisting the length to try to relieve the pleasure.

Nothing would stop other than a release. Tonguing her clit, he glanced up to see her tits shaking with her arousal.

Her cum coated his tongue, and he swallowed it down.

"Let go, baby. Feel the pleasure."

Reaching up, he fingered her nipples, pinching and twisting the hard nubs. She screamed out, climaxing on his tongue seconds later.

Nick flicked her clit, feeling her come apart against his mouth. She was shaking, quivering on the table.

Pulling away, he wiped her cream from his chin. He helped her to sit up. Gripping her hair in his fist, he tilted her head back to claim her full lips.

"You're so fucking beautiful. You will let me lick you whenever I want, do you understand?"

She nodded. Her eyes were wide. From the flush of her cheeks and the shaking of her body, he knew it was the first time she'd ever reached orgasm. Sitting back down on the sofa, he fisted his cock. "Now, we get back to your punishment," he said.

Clara swallowed, looking nervous.

"Yes."

He thought about her punishment. It would be so easy to take her over his knee and spank that full ass. Nick wasn't a Dominant, and he had more interesting ways of punishing his prize.

****

Clara's entire body was on red alert. The orgasm he'd given her had taken her completely by surprise. The feel of his tongue across her pussy had sent her arousal onto a level she wasn't anticipating.

"How should I punish you?"

He didn't expect a response, and she didn't give him one.

Her mind was all over the place. Nick was the first man to give her an orgasm. Closing her eyes, she pressed a hand to her stomach to try to stem the turmoil building within her. She wanted to hate him so much, but every second that she got to know him, her anger turned into something else.

"I know the perfect punishment."

Opening her eyes, she stared into his dark brown ones.

"Come here, Clara."

The sound of her name coming from his lips seemed more exotic and seductive somehow. It wasn't possible for a name to hold so much meaning, yet Nick made her think far more than what was actually there between them. He'd paid for her. She was merely a female for his pleasure.

Getting to her feet, she took the few steps to stand between his thighs.

"Straddle my lap. I want a leg on either side."

"I'm not ready to have sex," she said, panicking.

"When I'm ready to fuck you, you'll know it. Until then, do as I say."

She saw no use in arguing with him. Climbing onto his lap, she rested in an awkward position with her legs painfully tight to her body.

"Wrap your legs around my back." His hand moved between them. She felt the length of his cock against her pussy. "There, I'm not going to be fucking you today."

"What's my punishment?" she asked, feeling nervous. They were so close. She wasn't used to this kind of touching at all. Usually she wore clothes, and no one saw her naked. Not only had Nick seen her naked, he'd also brought her to orgasm.

"You'll see." His hands landed on her ass. Her breasts were pressed to his chest. She watched as his gaze moved down toward her chest. "Offer me one of your tits."

Lifting a breast up to his mouth she tensed at the first touch of his lips around her nipple. He sucked the red flesh inside, and she cried out at the pleasure shooting through her body going straight to her clit.

Nick moved onto the next breast taking his time to suck on her nipples and to kiss down her body.

His hands caressed up and down her back, cupping her ass to rub her pussy against his cock. The sensation he was causing was everywhere.

"I want you to grip my cock," he said, nibbling her flesh.

"What?"

"Grab my cock."

She'd never touched a man's parts before. Reaching down, she circled his cock with her fingers, trying not to touch him too tightly.

"More, hold me firmly, Clara, please."

Hearing the word please come from his lips surprised her. The little time they'd known each other he'd never used the word toward her.

Gripping his cock tightly she felt the heat of him against her palm. He cursed, throwing his head back. His gaze was on her. The dark amber of his irises looked more wolf than human.

"Do you have any idea what you're doing to me?" he asked.

She shook her head. Clara really didn't have a clue. Glancing down to his lips, she wanted to feel them on her skin once again. Something was happening to her. She should be fighting, but all she wanted to do was kiss him, be with him.

"Here, touch me like this," he said, circling her hand with his own. He showed her what he liked, the pressure of her hand as she worked up and down the length of his cock.

Clara couldn't look away from the glistening tip glinting up at her as she worked his cock. When he moved his hand away she kept up the action wanting to give him pleasure like he'd done her.

"Kiss me, Clara."

She glanced up to see him staring at her. Leaning forward, she kept up the movement of her fist. He didn't open up like she had to him. Both of his hands cupped her face before they dove into her hair, pulling on the length.

With her head pulled backwards, her breasts were

exposed.

"I'm not going to fuck you today, Clara. I will warn you I'll do a hell of a lot more to your body, but I will not fuck you. I don't need to have my cock inside you to bring us both pleasure." He kissed down her neck, biting over her pulse.

His touch was driving her crazy. What they were doing together was more than she could have ever hoped for. Working his cock she felt the wetness at the tip with each glide up then down. Crying out, she gazed down to see him sucking her breasts, taking each nipple in turn. Her body no longer felt like her own but was his to do with as he pleased.

Nick went from one breast to the other alternating between the two. He bit down, sucked then licked before turning his attention to the next.

"Harder, make it burn for me, baby," he said.

Tightening her grip, she cried out at the sudden jolt of pleasure slamming through her going straight to her clit. The grip in her hair tugged her head backwards. He kissed her neck going up to claim her lips then down to take her nipple.

She worked her hand harder and faster trying to send him over the peak like he'd done with her.

"Fuck, I'm going to come," he said, panting. His breath was deeper than she'd ever heard it. His hips jolted causing her to bounce on his lap. Glancing down she watched him move his cock, and the first wave of white cum spurted onto his stomach. Nick kept climaxing. His release coated their stomachs with each pulse. She was fascinated by what she'd done to him.

"Thank you," he said, seconds later when nothing else would come from him.

"Erm, you're welcome."

"Your punishment is over with," he said, drawing

her down to kiss her. "You may go and get changed now."

Staring down into his dark brown eyes, Clara frowned. "What? That's my punishment?"

"I could take you over my knee, but I thought your punishment was sufficient."

Clara didn't argue because as far as punishment went, it was the best one she'd ever experienced.

Chapter Six

Nick saw the shock on Clara's face along with the happiness. Slapping her ass, he ordered her to go and get dressed. Glancing down at his cum coated stomach he shook his head. He'd make a fucking awful Dom. When he walked into the sitting room he had every intention of slapping her ass. Seeing an opportunity to get more pleasure out of the experience had driven him to change the punishment to suit his need.

Getting up from the furniture he checked to make sure none of their releases had gotten onto the fabric.

Satisfied all was clear, he grabbed his clothing and walked to his bedroom. Showering and changing into a fresh set of clothes he went back downstairs to find Clara sitting in the robe once again.

"I've got to go out," he said, thinking about the urgent call from his office. "I'll be back for my guests. Amuse yourself, Clara. Look around, go for a swim. You can also stand around naked. No one will see you."

The light brightened in her gaze.

"You won't get a single chance to escape," he said. "I've coded everything. The moment I leave this house, the doors will close, and your only access outside will be looking through the windows." He saw the hope die within her.

He hated the sight of her defeat. Standing close to her, he leaned down kissing her head. "I'll be back before you know it."

The desire to stay at home was strong. He'd cut the conversation short and knew he had no choice but to go in.

"Amuse yourself while I'm gone."

Before he changed his mind, he spun on his heel and headed outside. The moment the door closed, all other doors and windows would shut. He'd designed the security for his own peace of mind. After being outlawed from all packs he'd been concerned for his safety. Some pack alphas would get it into their heads to hunt down an outlaw and remove him permanently.

No one even tried to hunt him down. They must all know he'd kill anyone who tried.

Climbing into his car, he waited for the gate to open then shut it before he was driving down the street heading toward the city to deal with his current problem. Getting a call from one of his security managers about Mark invading his offices had been a slight problem. Hearing from Mark again was another one of his problems mounting up the list of stuff he needed to deal with. The agreement should have been that their contact would cease the moment he paid for Clara.

Parking his car, he nodded toward another wolf shifter on his security team. Nick made sure to employ outlawed wolves like him. Most of the wolves didn't have the invasive mark that he did, but he respected them all the same.

He took the elevator taking him straight to his office. Dean was standing there with Mark and one of his security men, Bill.

"Get the fuck off me. This is business, nothing else," Mark said.

Closing the door, he watched with satisfaction as the men flinched. All of them had been so preoccupied with arguing they hadn't even smelled his approach.

"If I was still an alpha of a pack, I'd punish you all for simply not paying attention," Nick said, gaining their attention. Bill had walked out of his pack when they'd murdered his wife for being unfaithful to him. The laws of the pack were strict. Once a male and female mated, it was for life. If a female was to cheat then death was the penalty. He noticed the same rule didn't apply to the males. All they got was a slap on the wrist. Bill walked away because they took his life mate from him even though he'd asked to watch her with another man. Someone had spied on them, killed his mate, and Bill had left. The story was sad, depressingly so, and another reason why Nick would never be part of a pack even if one was offered.

"What's going on, Bill?" Nick asked, taking a seat behind his desk. Refusing to look at Mark, he concentrated on the men he didn't want to kill.

Don't kill her father. His death would make a mess, and there are more humans in the office than not.

He tried to reason with himself. The more he thought about what he learned of Clara, the harder it was not to hurt the bastard.

"This asshole," Bill said, pointing at Mark. "Stormed into your building shouting out his demands."

Bill looked ready to commit murder.

Get in line, Bill. Anyone who takes out this fucker will have to answer to me.

"He caused a stir, terrified the women, and started bad-mouthing you."

Moving his attention to Dean, he waited for another explanation.

"I tried to get him out of your office, Nick. He wants more money," Dean said, shrugging.

Getting his anger under control, Nick turned his attention onto the man he wished to murder. "What gives you the right to come into my place of work and start mouthing off?"

"I want more money."

"I paid you one million dollars for your daughter. You're not getting another cent from me." Staring at Clara's father, Nick couldn't stop the feeling of repulsion coming over him.

"She's worth a lot more than a million."

"I heard your wife say Clara is the runt of the litter. She means nothing to you. A million is more than fair." In truth, Nick would pay triple if not more to keep her.

"If you don't pay me more I'm going to the collection of alphas."

Nick raised a brow and turned to Dean, who shook his head.

"Interesting. You'll go to the collection of alphas?" Nick asked, standing up. The collection of alphas was responsible for his outlawed status. People referred to them as either the "collection of alphas" or as "the collective". The only desire he had to deal with the collective was to hurt them. The collection of alphas acted like social workers or the modern legal system for wolves.

"They would make you pay more."

"You really think they'd help you?" Nick asked, taking a step toward the other man. All he needed was any excuse to end this sack of shit's life and he'd do it in a heartbeat.

"I'm a pack wolf. They still answer to our calls, not outlawed bastards like yourself."

Leaning against his desk, Nick folded his arms over his chest, staring at the other man. "Go and get them. Tell them all that I won't pay you another cent of my money."

The other man looked confused. "I will."

"Good, then you can make them all aware how you sold a woman for money. Not only will you incriminate yourself, you'll bring everyone else down with you. I wonder how long you and your family would survive being outlawed with a lot of enemies, stronger enemies."

He let his words sink in.

"I'll get you for this," Mark said, pulling out of Bill and Dean's hold.

"I'm sure you will. Bye." Nick watched the angry man leave his office.

"Why does he suddenly want more?" Nick asked, turning to Dean.

"From what I hear he learned who you were and that you could pay a lot more money for her. He feels cheated that he only got so little from you instead of a larger payout."

"Fucking asshole." Nick made arrangements with Bill to increase security. Once he was alone, he dialed one of the security firms he trusted and put a man on to trail Mark. The last thing he needed was for him to turn up and ruin his plans to mate with Clara.

****

Walking around naked was not something Clara was ever going to be comfortable with. For so long she'd been forced to wear clothing that changing her habits was going to be hard. Hearing the door shut she stayed seated and watched the doors leading out of the kitchen to the patio close, beeping with a lock.

When she heard the gate close she stood up going toward the window. She tried to open one of the windows. None of them would move. The small draft came from a partially opened window near the ceiling. Unless she wanted to risk breaking her neck she wouldn't get through the slight gap.

Through the house she tried all the doors leading toward the outside. All of them were locked. She went to her room to try the door for the veranda, and once again she was stopped from going any further.

Great, she was locked in a large house with

nothing to do. Sitting down on the edge of the bed she blew out a breath. Tapping her legs, she glanced around the room looking for something to do.

I'm bored.

Looking up at the wall in front of her, she waited for some miraculous idea to come to her.

Nothing.

I'm bored.

Again with the tapping of her leg, looking around the room for something to do, she found nothing.

There was no need to clean either.

I'm bored.

Losing her temper, she stood up leaving the bedroom.

She was alone in a large house that resembled a mansion, and instead of running around having fun she was sitting on the bed, bored out of her mind. Poking her head out of the door, she looked up and down the hall.

Drawing in air, she let out an ear-piercing scream. The noise echoed around the large house. Leaving her bedroom, she jumped up and down losing her mind as she ran up and down the corridor. Opening every door she came to she stuck her head inside, taking a quick glance.

Back at home she wasn't allowed to do anything or make too much noise. Finally letting go in the freedom of the large house, she ran up and down the corridor, charging downstairs making a lot of noise. She screamed, yelled, and cursed out, loving every second of not fearing a beating.

Once she got out of breath and bored of running up and downstairs, she went into the kitchen.

In the fridge she found a selection of chocolates along with plenty of fresh vegetables and fruit. Grabbing the chocolate along with the carton of juice she left the kitchen behind. She would spend more time exploring the kitchen later. Her love of cooking would send her there in no time. At home she wasn't allowed to cook as her mother hated anything she did.

Clara walked into his office, checking out some of the books on his shelves. His collection was amazing. None of the books were romantic. She sat behind his desk staring at the laptop. Clicking open she saw it was protected by a password. Wrinkling her nose she left the juice and chocolates on his desk to continue her search.

Running fingers through her hair, she moved from room to room looking for something to do. His office was a bust. Watching television in the sitting room wasn't going to work. Every time she looked at the coffee table she saw his head moving between her thighs giving her more pleasure than she could ever imagine.

Swinging her arms backwards and forwards she walked toward the back of the house and opened a door to his gym. She checked over the running machine, weights and other pieces of equipment before following through the room to find a swimming pool. The water looked clear and beautiful. Bending down, she placed her hand in the water swooshing it around.

Sitting on the edge she put her legs into the water, kicking out.

She hadn't gone swimming in such a long time. Would it be so bad to take the time now?

Lifting the shirt over her head, she climbed into the water trying not to create too much of a ripple.

Kicking off she did the width of the pool before swimming lengthways.

The feel of the water was amazing. She did several lengths before lying on her back staring up at the ceiling.

Time passed, and Clara realized how happy she

actually was. When she was with her family she spent all of her time being scared in case she said something out of line to upset them. Constantly watching what she said or the way she looked had been exhausting. Nick didn't want anything from her, apart from her body. He wasn't making any demands.

Was it really so bad to be bought?

The anger she clung to evaporated as she thought about how good her life could be away from her family and the pack. They never loved her or cared about her. She'd been a thing of ridicule to them.

Something grabbed her around the waist. Screaming, Clara panicked and kicked out at the person who held onto her.

Kicking to the surface she spun to face him, and she saw Nick breaking the surface. He wasn't wearing a shirt, and her gaze wandered to the expanse of flesh on display.

"If I knew showing you the pool would get you naked I'd have done so this morning," he said, pushing hair off his face.

"You fucking scared me." Finding her anger, she slapped out at his chest. Her heart was racing, and it had nothing to do with wanting sex. Nick had scared her.

He must have seen her fear as he held his hands up. "I'm so sorry. I thought you'd hear me."

She'd been so lost in her thoughts she hadn't heard anything. He held her arms pulling her closer. Hitting him one final time she wrapped her arms around him.

"Shit, I'm so sorry. I didn't mean to scare you at all."

When she got her bearings back, she swam away, going to the other side of the pool.

Idiot. What the hell was all that about?

"How did you know where I was?" she asked.

"I followed your trail of crumbs. Those chocolates are expensive," he said.

"I was hungry."

"I'm not surprised. You should have eaten more this morning." He was close.

His hands went to either side of her blocking her against the side of the pool and his large body. She wouldn't turn around to look at him.

"If you let me get a job I can replace your chocolates."

"Not a chance. I don't care about the chocolates. They're yours. Everything in this house is yours."

Glancing over her shoulder, she saw him lean closer kissing her shoulder.

"I was bored," she said.

"What would stop you being bored?"

"Work."

He chuckled. "You're not getting a job, Clara. Try again."

Rolling her eyes she thought about what would keep her sane.

"Books."

"I've got plenty of books for you to read."

"Your taste in books is boring. I'm a woman, Nick."

"I know." His hands cupped her breasts making her gasp.

"I like romance books." Trying to focus on anything while he cupped her breasts was hard. Romance books, she needed romance books. *Focus on them.*

"Do you want paperbacks, or should I organize an e-reader?" he asked.

"What?"

"I can give you an account for your books, or I

can have an e-reader in your hands by the end of the day and you can order whatever the hell you like." He kissed her neck, sucking on her pulse once again.

Heat flooded her pussy.

"You'd do that for me?"

"I can't have my woman bored, now can I?" he asked.

She shook her head getting a thrill at his attention.

"Turn around and kiss me."

Clara spun around, wrapping her arms around his neck holding on. Pressing her lips to his she moaned at the contact.

His hands moved to her hair, tugging on the strands. She broke away from the kiss, closing her eyes as his lips descended. His lips and teeth bit her nipples.

She wanted more.

The sound of the doorbell going echoed around the house.

"How can we hear that?" she asked, jerking up expecting to see a lot more people entering the room.

"The house is big, and I need to be able to hear everything." His gaze fell back to her. "Saved by the bell."

He kissed her lips before climbing out.

Clara accepted his hand and got out alongside him. She wondered who was at the door. Her curiosity was the only reason. She refused to accept that she hated Nick being interrupted.

Grabbing her shirt, she followed behind him. Her emotions were all over the place. She didn't know what she liked or not.

Chapter Seven

Nick grabbed his trousers tugging them on as he walked out of the pool. He'd forgotten all about the delivery of Clara's clothes. Taking her hand they walked toward the front door. He left the gate open on his way inside.

The moment he entered the pool seeing her naked all of his plans left his mind. The only plan he had was to get Clara wrapped around him. Fuck, his cock was rock hard and causing him no end of trouble.

He opened the door and ushered the people toward the sitting room. "I want you to pick out whatever you want," he said.

His money spoke volumes, and he had been able to get the woman who owned a boutique in town to bring plenty of outfits for Clara to try.

"Where are you going?" she asked, nibbling her lip.

Shit, she was going to be the death of him.

"I've got to see a guy about an e-reader," he said.

Her smile was beautiful. Kissing her head, he ordered her to have fun. Going into his office, he dialed Dean's number.

"What can I do for you now?" he asked. "I gave you the means of getting a woman. What more could you possibly want?"

"I need you to pick up an e-reader and bring it to my house," Nick said, eating one of the chocolates left in the box. They really were tasty. He wondered if she liked them or not. There were not many left in the box. Sipping at the juice he stared out of the window.

"What the fuck for?" Dean was a lazy ass. He only ever did what was necessary and never went out of his way.

"I've got to find some way to keep my woman interested. I didn't buy her to remain on her back at all times." He took another chocolate waiting for his friend to answer.

"I can't stay for dinner. Pack is having a meeting and is requesting my presence." Dean's pack didn't like their friendship. Nick wondered if it was going to cause the other man a problem and asked. "It shouldn't. None of the packs should have any influence in being friends."

He heard Dean sigh. Their friendship was strange. They were both wealthy businessmen. Dean worked for him as well when it came to business with other wolves. They also had many ventures together making money.

"If it does let me know. I doubt you could handle exile."

"Fuck off, Nick. I could more than handle exile. I've got a string of willing women who'd come with me."

Laughing, Nick turned back to look through the door. Clara was turning in a pair of jeans that did nothing for her figure and pissed him off. In fact they were horrid. They made her look large without any curves. "I've got to go. Don't forget the e-reader, or I'll never forgive you."

"Whatever. See you soon." Dean rung off first. Snapping his phone shut, Nick went toward the other room.

"You're not having them. They're fucking horrid."

For the next hour he stopped Clara from taking clothes that were awful. When she made no move toward the dresses or skirt, Nick picked out the colors he liked. He stood watching her as she changed into the skirts. The women were sniggering, but he didn't give them any of his attention. His focus was entirely on the woman in front of him.

"Nick, please, turn around," she said, begging him.

"This is my hard-earned money. I'm not going anywhere, honey. You're going to change into the clothes I like." Tapping his chin, he waited for her to wriggle into the skirt. Staring at it with a critical eye, he picked out three pencil skirts along with ten dresses. "We'll go shopping soon for more clothes."

He packed the women out of his house leaving him alone with Clara. Turning around he saw Clara wasn't standing behind him. Nick found her folding up clothes and placing them in a neat pile. She tugged off the tags hanging from the neck of each item.

"What are you doing?" he asked.

"I'm putting my new clothes away," she said. Her agitation was easy to read.

"Why do I get the feeling you're pissed at me?" he asked.

She stood up, glaring at him but not saying a word.

"Am I supposed to guess what's going on in your head?"

Clara picked up the clothes and brushed past him. Staring up at the ceiling, Nick wished they were back in the pool when she was softer against him, loving what he did to her body. Checking his watch, he saw it was only a little after three. Dean wouldn't be arriving 'til six, and then they had the rest of the night. There was no way he'd be spending the rest of the day dealing with her mood.

Following upstairs, he found her putting clothes in the walk-in wardrobe. "What's your problem?" he asked.

"Nothing," she said, brushing him off. She

pushed past him to grab another item of clothing. For several minutes she busied herself ignoring him at every turn. His anger was increasing. She was supposed to be thankful to him. Not only had he bought her but he'd also given her a far better life.

"Stop." He grabbed her arm as she tried to pass him.

She stared at the ground, not giving him the time of day.

"For fuck's sake, stop being a baby and tell me what your problem is."

Her eyes sparkled, shooting him with a glare. He found her anger incredibly cute.

Not good. She's pissed.

"I'm being a baby? I'm not the one who has to be in control of everything." She growled out her frustration. Tugging her arm out of his hold, she finished putting away her clothing.

His frustration was piqued. "What the fuck are you talking about?" he asked.

"You have no idea, do you?"

"I'm not a bloody woman. I can't read minds either." Running fingers through his hair he was confused by what went wrong.

"Fine. It's all right for you being used to being this fucking god to all women, but people like me are not."

"What the hell are you getting at?" he asked.

None of her words were making sense. Why couldn't they go back to the pool where she was more than happy to give a part of herself to him?

****

Nick was going to make her say it. Clara folded her arms underneath her breasts aware the shirt she wore rode up her thighs. She had spent the last hour listening to the women laugh and giggle. Every noise made her aware of how she stood out like a sore thumb. He could have any woman he wanted. Instead he'd bought her.

Why would anyone want anything to do with her? The women were gorgeous and didn't have a single ounce of excess fat on them.

"What are you trying to say?" he asked, repeating his question.

"Why me? Why did you pick me?" She opened her arms wide feeling all the years of insecurity clawing up on her.

His eyes looked up and down her body. "Whatever you've got to say, Clara, just come out and say it," he said.

She knew he was angry, but so was she.

"I'm not like other women. I eat food, and I've got extra weight on my bones. I'm not beautiful at all. Why me? Why did you pick me?" she asked, glaring at him.

When she finished, she was panting for breath.

"You didn't learn anything from your punishment, did you?" His hands rested on his hips waiting.

"This morning wasn't about punishment. You were just looking for any excuse to get me naked. You're like them." She pointed downstairs thinking about how the woman left her feeling. "You only want to humiliate me."

Clara stared at him accusing him at every turn.

"So you think I only want to hurt you, humiliate you?" he asked.

"We don't know each other. What am I supposed to think?"

Nick took a step back. "I don't care what you think, but whatever it is, I need to get away from you, otherwise I'm going to hurt you."

He left the room, leaving her standing, staring at the space he'd been standing in.

What had just happened? Folding her arms, she held onto herself trying to ground her rioting thoughts. Shit, she'd just accused him of using her when the truth was she'd been angry and jealous of the women. When he left the room they'd talked amongst themselves ignoring her.

Why had she lashed out at Nick? He'd not done anything but make her feel special since knowing him. This morning had been the highlight of her life. His touch made her burn in ways she didn't know existed.

Great, Clara, you've fucked up big time.

Feeling awful at blaming Nick for everything, she started walking around the house trying to find him. He was nowhere to be seen. His office was bare along with the kitchen, sitting room and the garden. The doors were no longer closed. Her chance to escape was at her fingertips. Stepping out, she looked up at the sun feeling the heat glowing over her.

"No," she said, speaking to herself.

She couldn't leave.

Turning, she walked back into the house and went toward the gym. She found Nick pummeling the life out of a punching bag that hung on a hook. He didn't stop as she entered.

"You could have run," he said, hitting out.

"I know. I didn't want to leave." She answered him truthfully.

He jerked, turning to look at her. "Why? I'm such an awful person."

Staring down at the floor she wished it would open up and take her away. "I was an idiot."

Nick started to hit at the punching bag.

"I'm sorry, okay. I don't know you at all, and I lashed out. I shouldn't have done it, but I did." She ran fingers through her hair, looking around the room. "You bought me with money, Nick. What do you expect me to say?"

"I took you away from cruel bastards who were abusing you." His eyes shone amber as they stared at her.

"I don't know you. You're outlawed."

She'd seen the silver in his chest showing his outlawed status. The sight didn't affect or offend her. Clara recalled women saying how ugly it made the person who carried the outlawed mark. Nick wasn't ugly. Nothing would stop his sexiness, not even silver embedded in his chest.

He lashed out, kicking the punching bag off the hook. She watched the dent the bag made in the wall. His strength shocked her.

"You want to know about me, fine, I'll tell you what you need to know." He turned to stare at her.

She glanced down to his chest, biting her lip at the silver. It must have hurt to have his flesh cut apart and the silver poured into the cut.

"I was an alpha. A fucking good one. I ruled my pack and took pride at how they flourished. Every decision I made, I did so to bring them a good life. I'm not a mean son of a bitch like some of them." He picked up the bag, resting it against the opposite wall. She saw him shake his head at the damage he caused.

"Then one day I invited some of the alpha collective to my place in kindness and celebration of a mated couple." He stared at something over her shoulder, clearly seeing into his own past rather than at her. "The celebrations were high, the alcohol was flowing, the love building to a combustible level." He swallowed. "I walked into the house to hear screaming and scuffling.

The smell of fear came from the basement. Without calling for any of my pack I went to see what the damage was."

Tears filled her eyes at the memory he was creating. She didn't want to know what happened next but felt compelled to listen.

"I found the mated female dead on the floor. Her body was badly bruised, and one of the collective alphas was trying to clean up the mess of his rape and murder." Tears glistened in his eyes at the bitter memory. "I helped that girl. She had been part of my pack from a baby. I was there when she reached full maturity. The full moon was a festive reason to gather and enjoy." He stopped to bite his lip. "The alpha took that away from her. He forced himself on her, and before she could shout out, he killed her. Suffocated her until he was finished."

The sight must have been horrific, but to have known the woman would leave more scars that were worse than any kind on the flesh.

"He was an alpha, and he had hurt one of my females. I loved her like a daughter, and he ended her life because she refused him. I didn't seek justice from the others. I took care of my own justice. I killed him and gave his head to her mate as a prize." Nick took a step closer. "That's the kind of man I am, Clara. If anyone tries to hurt what's mine, I will exact my vengeance. I was tried and then outlawed."

"What happened to the man, the mate?" she asked.

"He killed himself. If they could outlaw a man for killing a rapist and murderer, it didn't leave him much hope. He thanked me in his final letter for giving him some kind of closure."

He stormed past her, leaving her alone to dwell in everything he said. Nick was a good man regardless of the fact he had bought her.

Chapter Eight

Nick stayed away from Clara after admitting the truth. For the next week he only saw her for breakfast and dinner. He left for work early only to return late at night to find his dinner keeping warm in the oven. The e-reader was in the top part of his desk. He still needed to give it to her.

His reluctance to be near her was ridiculous. Staring at his phone on his office desk, Nick wondered if he should call her. At night he snuck into her bedroom to hold her throughout the night. Come morning, he left her alone. She never said a word about him staying with her.

She tried to have conversations with him, but he cut her short, finding peace in another part of the house.

"You know, buying a woman was supposed to mean you'd stop being so bloody moody," Dean said, sitting opposite him.

"What?" Nick asked, jerking up to look at the other man.

"You're moody. Your employees are afraid to enter your office in case you have a go at them." Dean leaned forward taking one of the sweets, Nick left out.

"What the fuck are you doing in my office?" He wasn't in the mood to deal with his friend. The other man's perky attitude was not welcome. He needed to think.

"I got a call from your personal assistant, who is worried about you. She asked for me to come down and see you," Dean said.

"I should fire the woman." Mrs. Lambert was amazing. She put up with all of his quirks and never argued with him even though he deserved it half the time.

"Trouble in paradise?"

Glaring at him, Nick turned off his computer and

stood.

"Didn't the e-reader work?"

Ignoring his friend, Nick tried to think of an excuse to get rid of him. Even Dean took offence at being used and told him to fuck off.

"How was your meeting with the alphas?" Nick asked, getting ready to leave for home.

"Stop dodging my questions. You bought Clara. Why are you looking moody? I thought the point of her was for you to let off steam."

Nick didn't say anything.

"For fuck's sake, stop cutting everyone off. Talking actually helps. I know it's strange for you to even consider shit like that, but it does fucking work," Dean said.

"I told her why I was outlawed. I lost my temper with what she said and told her everything. We've not spoken in the last week. To be honest, I don't have a clue what to say to her or how to move past what I've said." He shrugged, feeling lost for the first time in his life. When he was being sentenced to be outlawed, he hadn't felt lost. All of his life he'd known everything there was to know about his pack. Clara made him feel lost at every turn.

"Shit, what did she say?" Dean asked.

"I haven't given her chance to say or do anything. I won't say anything, and I don't know what to do in order for us to start talking."

Dean was silent for several seconds.

"Where are you going?"

"I'm going home. I try to find ways to break the ice, but I stop before I get the chance to mend our fences."

He walked toward the door. Dean was one of the few men he actually trusted.

"Give her the e-reader," Dean said, catching his attention again.

"What?"

"You bought her the damn thing. Give it to her over dinner tonight and start talking. I don't know. Sit with her while she downloads books. Don't give up."

Nick would certainly think about it. He'd love the chance to hold her in his arms before she fell to sleep.

"What happened with the alphas?" he asked, interested to know what was going on in the world he'd left behind.

"They're talking about the selling of women. They've stumbled onto the websites along with the auctions of female wolves. They're not happy and are asking for my help."

"I take it I was mentioned."

"Yes, but more as a topic of interest, Nick. I believe they regret outlawing you."

"Well, they did, and there's no going back. I'll see you soon," Nick said, ready to leave.

"If they were to offer you back your status and give you a pack, would you take it?" Dean asked.

"No, I wouldn't." Nick didn't hesitate in answering. In the early days of becoming an outlaw he'd have taken his pack back at the first moment. Now, he wouldn't dream of going back. They could give him back his pack and easily take it away.

"Why not?"

"I no longer want a pack that's overruled by a collective of alphas who think they're above the law."

"It was a long time ago, Nick. You've got to get over one man's actions." Dean placed a comforting hand on his shoulder. He shrugged the hand off.

"You didn't see what he did to her. If you did, you wouldn't be trying to bring me back into the fold.

My life as an alpha ended that day." Nick walked out of the office, thankful to leave his past behind.

Clara knew the truth, and it was time for him to man up. It wasn't her fault he still felt guilty for putting the female in harm's way.

The drive home didn't last long enough. He entered the house and heard Clara making something in the kitchen. The scent of her baking filled the house. He noticed she baked a lot. Nick had taken her spare baking into the office so none of it went off.

He couldn't be that moody to share his woman's baking, could he?

Either way, he went to his office, putting his case away then grabbing the e-reader from the desk. It was all set up ready to receive books.

Give it to her.

She used to meet him the moment he walked into the house after he shouted at her. After the third day of him yelling at her, she stopped welcoming him home.

He'd fucked up. Keeping hold of the e-reader, Nick was determined to fix what he'd broken.

****

Clara kept mixing the potatoes even as she heard Nick enter the house. She had fucked up and hadn't gotten the opportunity to apologize to him. There was only so much shouting she could deal with, so she tried to stay out of his way. She tried not to feel the hurt of being cut off from all contact. The last week with Nick had been the same as living with her parents. He didn't talk to her, only accepted silence, and she spent most of her time trying to avoid him. The latest batch of cookies was cooling on the tray.

The only consolation she found was him taking her baking into work. At least nothing went off. She found the cookbooks in one of the cupboards, and her days had been spent marking the pages of the recipes she wanted to cook. He never complained about what she cooked, nor did he voice happiness at the food she presented to him.

The chicken and roast potatoes were keeping warm, and she tasted the mashed potatoes to see for their seasoning. Once they were done, she walked into the dining room to set their places.

When that was done, she went and served up. Putting the two plates on the mats, she removed the apron she used to keep her clothes nice and clean.

She wore a pair of tight jeans and red shirt that molded to her curves. Licking her lips, she pinched her cheeks hoping to put some color back into them. Seconds later she knocked on his office door, which was closed.

"What?" he asked.

Shrinking away from his anger, she called through the door hoping he heard.

"Dinner is served," she said, moving away before he answered. Her place setting was beside him. Moving it three chairs down like the other times she took a seat and started to eat.

Clara refused to cry at his harsh words.

He joined her, stopping beside her chair. She stayed tense wondering if he would send her away. Holding her breath, she waited for him to move before eating again.

She sped up eating in the hope of getting away from him quickly.

"How was your day?" he asked.

"Fine."

Nick asked her, and when she started talking and talking, he demanded she shut up as he was only hoping for a one word answer. He started eating, and Clara finished, leaving half of her plate. His anger unnerved her more than anything else.

Taking her drink with her, she entered the kitchen and started cleaning up. It was stupid of her trying to look nice for him. Whatever they'd shared in the first twenty-four hours of them knowing each other was long gone.

She washed up by hand each item. Twenty minutes had passed by the time she finished with the kitchen. Nick should be finished and long gone to his own part of the house giving her the freedom to disappear to her room.

Entering the dining room she found Nick sat, staring at the door. His gaze was on her, and she froze.

"Are you finished?" she asked.

"No, come and sit with me."

"I've got to finish the dishes." She took a step back ready to escape.

"I've just listened to you do all the dishes and take your time about it. I'm sure my plate can wait for you to wash. I'm not covered in diseases."

She blushed and stepped closer to take her seat.

"No, don't sit there. Sit here." He shoved the chair beside him out for her to sit on.

Once she was seated, she locked her fingers together in her lap.

"I've been a complete bastard to you, and I apologize."

Staying silent, she chanced a look at him. His eyes were on her and made no move to look away.

"Erm, what do you want?" she asked after several seconds when he didn't speak.

"Will you accept my apology?"

"There's nothing to accept. I overreacted, and I wanted to say sorry to you."

"No, you didn't overreact at all, but I accept your

apology." He took her hand, locking their fingers together. Staring at where he touched her to his face, Clara felt her heart racing. This was the first real contact they had in over a week. "I shouldn't have treated you the way I did. I hope you can forgive me."

She nodded. "I forgive you."

"You're not going to make me grovel?"

"No."

"Well, I've got a present for you. I had intended to give you this a week ago." He leaned down and grabbed something off the floor.

Clara couldn't deny the excitement. He was the first person to think to give her a gift. "I don't own any romance novels, but I hope this can make up for it." He handed her a rectangular box.

Staring down at it she saw it was an e-reader.

"We can fill it up now if you want."

"Yes, I'd love that."

She opened the box easing out her present. The instructions were easy, and Nick got up, taking her hand as they headed toward his office. He took a seat then told her to sit on his lap. She was still tense but watched as he logged into his account.

Bringing up the books she started to pick out everything she wanted. After ten books she stopped, feeling embarrassed for asking for so much.

"You've not bought a lot. You're going to need enough to last you for the next week, Clara. Buy as much as you want."

He bought her over fifty books to get started. His hand rested on her back while she leaned forward reading blurbs and looking at the books she wanted to buy.

When she downloaded them all, she reached back and kissed his lips.

"Thank you," she said.

Nick caught the back of her neck, holding her in place. "Don't mention it." His fingers caressed the back of her neck. She still felt tense at his touch.

"I fancy going for a swim. Will you join me?" he asked.

She had a swimsuit with all of her clothes. "Sure."

"Good, I'll meet you in the pool." He slapped her ass lightly as she stood up.

Clara didn't look back and continued upstairs to change. She put her present beside her bed looking forward to reading the many books on the machine.

Removing her clothes, she quickly put her swimsuit on and went downstairs. She found the pool empty and dove into the water. Breaking the surface, she kept working her body in the hope of relieving some of the stress from her tight muscles.

Chapter Nine

Clara's tense body didn't go unnoticed to him. Nick finished paying for her purchases and stood to look outside of the window. He needed to put her at ease around him once more. His attitude over the past week would upset anyone even a fully grown man, and he'd directed it at Clara. She'd been the receiver of much unhappiness from her family, and all he'd done was add to it.

He hated the feeling of causing her pain. After enough time had passed he went to the pool. She was walking up and down the pool. He saw the tightness of her body from where he stood.

Hating every second she was nervous knowing he was the cause he removed his clothing. He left his boxer briefs on just in case. Clara no longer trusted him, and it was up to him to start to mend their fences. She'd tried and got her head bitten off for her attempt.

"I like your swimsuit," he said, drawing her attention toward him.

"It was with all the clothes you bought." She sank beneath the water hiding her body. Climbing inside he moved toward her, keeping each step steady.

"It looks good on you. I prefer you naked."

She turned and started to swim away from him. Cursing, Nick watched her go. They needed to cut through this stalemate somehow.

"Will you give me a fucking chance?" he asked, shouting when he didn't intend to. She stood up, turning to look at him.

The hurt in her eyes cut him deep.

"I told you the truth about how and why I became outlawed. Since then I've been a fucking idiot, and I regret my actions." He splashed the water feeling helpless. At least she stopped swimming to listen to him. "Please, talk to me."

"I tried to talk to you after you told me everything. You wouldn't listen to me."

"I know. I fucked up, okay. I was hurt, and I don't talk about my past with everyone. It still hurts to think about what happened. I don't care about not being an alpha, but knowing I failed my pack, still fucking hurts."

Nick decided to be honest with her rather than lie. She would understand or at least try to.

"I'm sorry you were outlawed. You sounded like a good alpha. You shouldn't have been cast out for what you did."

"I tried to be good to my pack. I'd do anything for them, even die for them if they asked." He opened his arms wide, looking around the pool. "When I bought you, I did it because I wanted to fuck a female wolf. I've been with hundreds of women, and none of them can take what I can give. I love hard sex, rough sex." He ran fingers through his hair as he put himself on the line. "I know I'm asking for a lot, but all I want is your forgiveness, Clara. I fucked up, but I don't just want sex from you. I want it all even though I don't deserve shit from you."

"Why don't you deserve anything from me?" she asked.

"I killed someone." He no longer cared he was a murderer. Over the years since it happened he had revisited that night over and over again and realized he wouldn't change a damn thing.

Any man who forced themselves and then killed a woman deserved to die in his book. His pack was his life, and protecting every member ran within his veins.

"You did it because he hurt one of your family. A

pack is supposed to be your family. I don't think badly of you, Nick. I admire your strength and your courage."

She stepped closer. He forced himself to stay still, giving her more than enough room to pad the water toward him.

"Not only did you exact your own justice, you gave her mate some peace of mind. He killed himself, but before they gave you such an awful sentence, he wouldn't have. You're not responsible for his death. The collective of alphas are."

Nick took her hand as she got close enough to touch. "You're too damn nice for your own good."

Clara smiled. "No, I'm not. I just know what it's like to not belong. My whole family hated me, Nick. Your pack loved you. Would you ever go back to them if given the chance?"

"No, I wouldn't." He couldn't bring himself to join back to a pack who'd been ruled by a different alpha for so long. That kind of takeover could cause more problems than he cared to think about.

Cupping the back of her neck, he drew her close.

"Why not?" she asked, whispering the words against his cheek.

"Taking over any pack can be tricky. Men, women, even the children know you're there because you overthrew their old alpha. I can't do that. I can't go back and see my pack hate me." Nick closed his eyes, more interested in inhaling her sweet scent. Fuck, the last week had been torture. Now that he had her in his arms, he never wanted to let go again. She meant everything to him.

"It was your pack to start off with. How can you not see them welcoming you with open arms?" She cupped his face, tilting him back to look at him.

Nick, given the choice, would have claimed her

mouth to silence her. He knew she deserved the truth.

"They put up a fight over the verdict, but they could do nothing. The alpha who took over is a good one. I made sure for the first couple of years that he was good for them all. I would never have forgiven myself if something happened to them." Nick hated it when he agreed with the new alpha's methods. When he realized he was never going to become an alpha again he had focused all of his attention into making money. Once he settled on money he made sure to employ other outlawed males who didn't agree with the collective alphas' decisions. His business thrived, and he'd found a best friend in Dean.

Life was more than perfect for him.

"Are you happy?" she asked.

Nick ran his fingers down her back to cup her ass. "With you in my life, Clara, I've never been happier." He turned her, pressing her against the side of the pool. His desire rose with every second passing. There was a challenge he needed to win. By the next full moon Clara would be in his bed.

Will you be in her heart?

Leaning down, he licked a line across her plump, inviting lips. The thought made him pause for a split second, wondering if it was possible to get her to fall for him. He'd bought her like a possession, and it was how he thought of her at times, his prized, virgin possession.

"Nick," she said, moaning.

"Do you forgive me?"

"Do you promise never to be a grouch again?"

"Yes." He claimed her lips, slamming his tongue inside her mouth. Nick trapped her against the wall, kissing her deeply, wanting her to moan and writhe against his touch.

She held onto his shoulders with her nails digging

into his flesh. He moaned, loving the small bite of pain her nails gave him.

Opening her thighs, he got her to wrap her legs around his waist. Her pussy pressed to his stomach, and he wished she'd not worn a one piece swimsuit. No matter, he'd have her naked in no time.

Cupping her ass, he gripped the back of her head holding her in place to take his kiss.

He broke the kiss first, going down her neck. Tearing the costume from her body, he exposed one full, rounded red nipple. Biting down into the harsh bud he heard her scream. The scent of her need wasn't dulled by the water.

Nick needed more. Walking toward the stairs at the far side of the pool he laid her on the cool ground.

In two easy tugs he removed the swimsuit from her body. He admired every curve, loving the feel of her against his palm.

"I will never regret owning you, Clara. I want you more than my next breath."

"Please, don't stop, Nick." She arched up as he sucked her nipple into his mouth. He tweaked the other nipple, watching her scream. Clara always responded to him when he caused just a slight edge of pain.

He worked his boxer briefs down and fisted his rock hard cock. The need built to a fever pitch inside him. Kissing down her body, he felt her stomach quiver beneath his touch.

When he got to her pussy he discovered she was blisteringly hot with copious amounts of cum getting her nice and slick for his cock.

Nick inhaled the musky scent of her cum before moving down to tongue her juicy slit. "Fuck, baby, you're so fucking ready for my cock."

Sliding his tongue down her pussy, he flicked her

clit feeling her shake at the slightest touch. She was so fucking sensitive.

"Please, Nick, I need you."

"Are you sure, baby?" He was more than ready to fuck her, but he hoped she was ready to take him.

Once he started he wasn't going to stop.

****

"Yes, I'm sure. Totally sure." Clara couldn't deny her need for him. She'd never been with a man before, and she trusted Nick to be her first. The last week had been a nightmare. Nick refusing to talk to her had left her feeling like she was back at home. After one day of feeling like a person who mattered, his lack of attention hurt more than ever. He was nothing like her family. The way he made her feel was more than she ever thought was possible.

Years of her family making her feel like a runt with her excess weight and ugliness had really dented her confidence.

He gripped her thighs, opening her wide. His tongue slid up and down her slit, smashing against her clit. The pleasure of his mouth was more than she could stand. There was nothing for her to hold onto. The ground beneath her was slick from the water of the pool. Closing her eyes, she thrust up to meet him feeling the first stirrings of her orgasm.

Nick held her down with a hand on her stomach. He kept her in place as he tormented her body. His talented tongue kept her at the edge of bliss but didn't allow her to tumble over. Crying out in frustration she didn't know what to do to make him give her an orgasm.

He reared up over her, breaking complete contact.

She stared into his eyes seeing the dark brown depths had changed to a light amber. His wolf was close to the surface. The heat radiating off him filled her with so much need.

"Please, Nick."

"I'm going to fuck you now, and when I'm done you're never going to think of another man." His words were strange considering he was the only man she ever wanted.

Glancing down, she saw him grip his arousal, rubbing the tip through her slit. He hit her clit, and she cried out at the explosion of pleasure.

"This is going to hurt, but I can't stop. Fuck, I can smell how horny you are. You need my cock." He fit the tip of his cock against her entrance. Already she felt him stretching her. The feeling wasn't entirely unpleasant either.

She kept begging him, wanting to feel his length within her.

His hands returned to her hips, holding her in place as with one hard thrust, he seated himself deep within her core. Clara screamed at the abrupt pain gripping her.

"Hold onto me, Clara. This pain can't be helped."

Tears filled her eyes, but she didn't struggle away from him. Clara did as he instructed, holding onto him as he held her in place. There was nowhere else for her to go other than in his arms. She needed him. The pain didn't last long and was soon overridden with intense pleasure.

The feel of his cock pulsing inside her gave her more pleasure than she ever imagined.

"Do you feel what you do to me?" he asked, pushing strands of errant hair out of the way. Nick kissed her lips, wiping away the tears that spilled out of her eyes. "You're so beautiful. You will never see what I do." He bit into her bottom lip, making her moan. Arching up against him, she felt his cock slide deeper within her core. "Your cunt is so slick and gripping me like a fucking fist."

His words turned her on.

"I should have taken your virginity in a bed, but I couldn't wait any longer. I needed to be inside you."

"Shut up and kiss me." She pressed a finger to his lips wanting him to stop. His cock was no longer hurting her but tormenting her. "Please, fuck me, Nick."

She'd read so many words of love and begging for sex in her books, never expecting to use them herself. Nick had made it all possible. Clara was so grateful to him for buying her. The very thought of why she was grateful made her want to laugh. No woman should be grateful for being bought.

"As my lady wishes." He took her lips before drawing out of her body. She whimpered, not wanting him to leave her at all. "Trust me, baby. I'm going to make you scream before the end."

Smiling, Clara more than trusted his ability to do as he said.

He drew all the way out of her until only the tip remained. "Look at us, Clara."

Glancing down, she saw the length of his cock with her cream along with a small tinge of blood on his cock. Heat flamed in her cheeks at the obvious evidence of arousal. "I'm going to fill you with my cum, Clara, and no man will ever touch you. I'm going to rub my scent into your fucking skin."

"Yes," she said, moaning.

Nick slammed in deep, hitting her cervix. The pain had her jerking off the floor. He merely caught her, pulling out and doing the same again. He fucked her hard, making each thrust hurt but also drove her closer toward her orgasm.

"Hold onto me."

She wrapped her arms around his neck, and he turned their positions so she was sitting on his lap. His cock was in as deep as it could go from this new angle. "I want to hold you and watch you come apart in my arms."

Acting on instinct, she kissed his lips. His fingers tightened in her hair, pulling her head back to expose her neck.

"There is so much I'm going to do to you," he said. His gaze fell to her breasts. "I'm going to bring you nothing but pleasure, Clara. Every step you take, you're going to be so sore and remember everything I do to you." He leaned down, taking one of her nipples into his mouth. "I'm going to fill your body with my cum and surround you with my scent."

He circled her nipples with his tongue then bit into them.

"You're driving me crazy," she said, gasping. He touched her clit, and her muscles tightened around his cock. His length felt bigger than ever before.

"Do you want me to let you come?" he asked.

"Yes."

She wouldn't last if he didn't let her come.

Chapter Ten

Nick stroked Clara's swollen clit. She was so fucking wild in his arms. The sight of her virgin blood on his cock had set off something primal inside his head. He wanted to surround her in his scent. For the rest of his life he would be pumping his seed deep into her body. He hadn't used a condom as it wasn't her time to conceive but also because he wanted her naked heat around his cock.

Every stroke over her clit had her cunt tightening around him like a fist. Her pussy was pure heaven. He'd never known such a tight pussy in all of his life. The moment he hit her cervix, he'd scented her pain along with the pleasure. She was so right for him.

His teeth started to elongate ready to mate with her. Dropping his head to her neck, licking the pulse that pounded against his tongue, Nick knew she wasn't ready to be mated to him. If he tried to mate her, she'd panic. The knowledge sent his teeth back until they were his human teeth once again.

Pinching her clit he thrust inside her, going deeper inside. She rode his cock as the pleasure took over. Clara panted for breath, and each sound coming out of her was of a moan. Her whole body was aflame and flushed.

"Please, Nick, please." Her begging pulled at him.

Pounding inside her Nick stroked her clit at the same time. Her body was shaking, and her cum surrounded his cock.

His own release was seconds away, but he wasn't going to come until she had.

"Come for me, Clara. Give me your cum."

She screamed as her orgasm struck her hard. He

fucked her hard, not quite so hard due to the angle, but hard enough to draw her pleasure out even more.

Nick held her tightly as he fucked to his own release. Grunting, he held her in place with an arm around her waist and another in her hair. She didn't try to shove away from him but held him tightly. They were both sweating as he pumped his cum into her waiting cunt.

"Fuck, baby, you're going to wear me out," he said, resting his head against hers.

"Me? This was all your fault." She rested against his shoulder.

Stroking her red hair, he felt each spasm of her pussy around him.

"I'm not a virgin anymore." She spoke the words in a sigh. Nick tensed. He'd tried to make it good for her through the pain.

"Do you regret being with me?"

"No." She pulled back. Her eyes were a sparkling green, and her face was a lovely rosy red. "It was the best feeling in the world." She kissed his lips, smiling. "Can we go again?"

"Soon." He picked her up looking at the pool. No, he wasn't going to wash in the pool. Nick carried her out of the pool, through the gym then out to the main hall before taking her upstairs to his room.

"Where are we going?" she asked, pressing her head against his.

"We're going to have a bath with some soothing salts to help with any soreness you may be feeling."

"Then can we fuck?"

The word sounded odd coming from her lips. Chuckling, he kicked open his bedroom door, carrying her over the threshold. "Have you ever said that word before?"

"Not really. I've read about it plenty." He placed her on her feet before setting about getting her into the bath.

He scented her virgin blood, and the urge to take care of her struck him hard.

Once the bath was filled with the soothing bath salts, he ordered her to rest.

"Where are you going?" she asked, grabbing his hand stopping him from leaving.

"I've got to get you something to help." He kissed her hand, sinking his fingers into her hair. "I'm not going anywhere. Tomorrow morning you'll thank me for my attention."

Stroking her cheek, he left the room walking back to the kitchen. He set some milk into a saucepan. Nick worked his kitchen while he was still naked. After sex clothing would have itched his skin. Opening a window he let the cool air into the room.

The smells of the fresh grass, the air and trees called to his wolf. The urge to leave the house and take a run of victory was strong. He forced the need down. Not only had he gotten Clara into his bed before the allotted time, he'd also found his mate.

Nick was sure she was his mate. The women he'd been with before had never inspired the mating bite within him.

Adding a splash of vanilla he gave it a whisk before adding the best chocolate he could find. Carrying hot chocolate, fruit, and cream, he went back upstairs to find her lying back resting.

"You're back?"

"I was tempted to go for a run, but I thought you might like to come with me." He climbed into the bathtub, putting the drinks on the floor along with the bowls of fruit and cream.

Once he was comfortable, he grabbed her cup and handed it to her.

"Is this supposed to help?" she asked.

"Nothing medicinal about it. I thought chocolate was the cures for all ills for women."

Clara chuckled. "Nah, it doesn't help at all, but the thought is perfect all on its own."

He watched her sipping at the liquid. Her plump lips were bruised from his kisses.

Reaching down, he grabbed a strawberry and dipped the ripe fruit into the cream. "Open up," he said, pressing the tip to her lips. Some of the cream dripped onto her breast. Clara bit into the fruit, and he finished it off.

"So juicy."

He leaned forward licking off the droplet of cream. "I agree, however, I know something else that is juicy." Nick raised a brow so she knew what he was talking about.

For the next twenty minutes he fed her fruit and cream as they finished off their hot chocolates. The bath water was cold by the time they were finished.

Nick climbed out first, grabbing a towel to wrap around her. Lifting Clara into his arms he carried her through to his bedroom.

"Am I going to my own room?" she asked.

"Not a chance." He couldn't resist her any longer. Sinking his fingers into her wet red hair, he tugged her close. "You're not going anywhere. This is your room from now on."

****

Nick's possessive attitude turned her on. The way he gripped her hair had Clara melting. She would have sunk to his feet begging for him to take her if he hadn't taken control. With his free hand, he gripped her waist holding her close.

In one quick move he spun her around so she faced away from him. His hands gripped her stomach, running up and down her body. "Your curves are so fucking addictive." Down his hands went gripping her thighs then up to cup her breasts. "I love your tits. You've got to know how amazing you are, Clara. Any man would feel special having you in their lives or in their bed. No one is going to know what it's like being inside you."

He moved her forward, pushing her to her knees on the bed. Over his bed was a mirror for her to see him. It wasn't long enough to see everything he was doing. His hands stroked her back, opening her thighs to suit him.

She felt the tip of his cock stroking through her slit before pausing at her entrance.

"Look at me, Clara," he said, tugging on her shoulder. She looked at him through the mirror. The moment her eyes were on him, he slammed inside her going far deeper than he had upstairs. "Fuck, you feel so good."

His eyes were a shade of amber once again, sparkling as they looked at her. The rippling of her body should have unnerved her, but the presence of his alpha wolf only turned her on more.

"Tell me to fuck you, Clara."

"Fuck me, Nick," she said.

With his gaze on her he pounded away inside her taking her breath away. Every time she closed her eyes, he slapped her ass forcing her to look at him.

"Don't close your fucking eyes. I want you to watch me fuck you."

Biting her lip, she cried out with each slap to her ass.

"Your ass is going to be fucking red if you don't stop."

The pleasure was more than she could stand.

"Touch your clit, Clara. Let me feel you come all over my cock."

Over and over he rammed inside her, hitting her cervix, which took the pleasure into a different dimension of pleasure and pain.

"So fucking tight and perfect."

She touched her clit, stroking the nub. Each stroke had her gasping.

Nick held onto her shoulders making her look at him even though she was close to coming.

"Keep those eyes on me, baby."

Where he held her there would be bruises.

"Please, Nick."

"Come over my cock and I'll put an end to both of our agony."

Whimpering, she fingered her clit feeling every jerk and pulse of his cock within her depths. He stretched her with each pound.

"You better get used to me inside you, baby. I'm not going anywhere. Your pussy is going to have my name all over it."

His words set off her climax, not to mention the addictive smell coming off his skin. Before he'd been outlawed, Nick had been an alpha. The alpha within him hadn't disappeared at all. In fact, it looked like he'd only gotten stronger, more powerful.

Clara exploded on his cock stroking her nub to completion. She felt the difference inside him. The instant she came his strokes became harder, his cock pressing against her cervix and determined to go deeper. The pain was intense along with how amazing it felt, so she didn't know whether to scream or cry with pain.

Nick pounded inside her until with a growl he came. His cock jerked, pulsing his cum inside her. She dropped to the bed needing her strength. Her shoulders ached from the strength of his arms.

When his orgasm subsided, he picked her back up, pulling his cock out of her.

"Where are we going?" she asked, wanting to curl up and sleep.

"We're going for a run."

She held onto him as he led her outside.

Staring across his grounds, she realized no one would ever be able to see inside his home it was that large.

"Aren't you afraid of me running off?" she asked.

"Are you going to run off? If you come back I can promise you everything. I can give you sex and anything your heart desires."

He couldn't give her everything. There was a reason she read so many romance novels, and it wasn't because it was what women did. She read them out of yearning. The books were her one way of getting a happy ending. In life she had come to learn it doesn't always have a happy ending.

"I'll come back," she said.

The sex between them was brilliant. She never wanted the lust to end. Clara wondered how long the brilliant sex would last without love. She'd seen many couples within her pack mate, then regret their decisions afterward.

Wolves were supposed to mate for life. Nick hadn't bought her to mate with. He'd only bought her for sex, and he was getting that without any fuss.

Stop thinking too much. Love has never entered the equation, and it shouldn't now.

She watched him shed his skin and become a

wolf. Heat filled her core at the sight of his amazing dark amber wolf. He waited for her to become a wolf. Staring up at the sky she closed her eyes and turned into her wolf.

When she turned with her old pack, their thoughts were always hurtful, which was why she'd always tried to run away from them.

"You're so beautiful. I should have known your wolf would be a dark red color."

Clara took off away from him.

"You're red all over, baby."

"Stop it and run."

"Whatever my lady wishes."

He ran beside her. The fresh air, along with the scent of the surrounding woodland, was heady. Her body was different, no longer innocent. The freedom to run without fear of what others said made the whole experience amazing.

"This is your life, Clara."

"I know."

He nudged her with his snout. *"No, this is your life. The freedom to run when you wish. I'll be with you every step of the way."*

"What are you saying?"

"Stay with me, willingly, and I'll give you everything your heart desires."

Clara cut off all hope. With them both in their wolf forms Nick would be able to hear her feelings of hope when it came to their relationship.

"Okay, I promise, I won't leave or run away."

She'd give them a chance.

Chapter Eleven

Nick leaned back in his office chair smiling. Another week had passed since he'd claimed Clara's virginity. Every morning he woke her up either licking her pussy or fucking her. She never complained, giving him everything he required. When he got home at night, he was met with a warm, naked, welcoming female and a good meal. He'd also stopped trapping her within the house. When he left the doors and windows open he'd spent the day at the office panicking in case she left him.

Clara had surprised him with lunch at the office. Since then, he loved waiting for her to visit him. Today, he was too fucking horny. The following week was the full moon, and he was in the mood to fuck. Most of his thoughts were focused on the ability to fuck. His cock was in a constant state of hardness even when she wasn't around. Clara didn't help. She was as bad as he was when it came to sex.

There were a few times he woke up to find her sucking him off. The woman was insatiable, and he was more than happy to let her experiment on him. He caught her watching the porn channel as well. If he reaped the rewards, he really didn't care.

Checking the time, he saw she'd be arriving in ten minutes. Buzzing his personal assistant he ordered her to keep Clara waiting but to let him know she arrived.

He returned his attention to the computer screen, reading through the latest email of a company he bought. Work was not interesting to him at all, but he forced himself to get through it. Clara turned up within ten minutes, and he scented her need for him as well. Licking his lips, he waited a few minutes before going to his door.

She sat in one of the waiting chairs. Her smile was a thing of beauty when she turned it toward him.

Nodding at his personal assistant he led Clara into his office. Closing and locking the door, he put the basket of food on the floor and pinned her against it.

"You took too fucking long," he said, sliding a hand underneath the yellow summer dress she wore. He found her naked flesh, no panties to stop his search.

"Please, Nick, I need you."

Waiting was not on his agenda. His cock was threatening to burst from his trousers. Lifting her up, he steadied her ass with a hand holding her there. "Undo my pants and pull my cock out."

He kept hold of her as she started to work free his trousers. Her hands were shaking, but she got him out.

Taking over, he pushed her hands out of the way and ordered her to hold up her dress. Nick found her wet heat, fit the tip of his cock to her pussy, and glided in easily. She groaned, and he covered her mouth to stop her from making too much noise. His personal assistant wasn't a wolf, but he did work with men who'd be able to hear her.

Stepping to the right, he pulled out of her heat to slam back inside. They were no longer against the door, and the wall would muffle the sounds of her pleasured cries.

She licked his palm. He kept her mouth covered as he fucked her tight pussy. No matter how many times he took her, she always seemed tighter than ever before.

"Pull your tits out for me to see."

Her arousal was driving him wild. There was no control over his response to her. She took all of his cock.

Every ripple had him panting for more.

"So fucking tight and wet," he said, pounding away.

She held onto his shoulders, growing closer to her own orgasm.

"Touch yourself, stroke your clit, baby. Let me feel you come all over my dick."

He felt her fingers stroking between them. When he got home tonight he would make her finger her sweet pussy on the coffee table while he watched. The night was all their own after dinner. Nick wanted to try some other things with her.

The instant her cunt tightened around him, Nick found his own release exploding within her. His scent filled her along with his cum. Any male wolf would know she belonged to another male.

When he was finished pouring his seed into her waiting body he helped her to her feet.

His seed escaped, and he grabbed some tissues from his desk to clean most of the mess away. She stayed still as he attended to her.

"How is your day?" he asked.

Clara laughed. "Shouldn't you have asked me that before you screwed me against the door?"

Nick laughed. He loved hearing the sound of her happiness. "I screwed you against the wall, not the door. I imagine I'd have embarrassed us all. I don't want to test the strength of the door."

"I can see that." She took a seat opposite his desk with her lunch basket in her lap. "I went shopping with the card you left me."

"Where did you go?" he asked.

He had also given her the codes to buy books online. Yesterday he found a three figure bill from her purchase of books alone. Nick wasn't going to complain. Many women wouldn't have been satisfied unless they were given jewelry.

"I went to the supermarket, looked at the meat

and hated the sight and smell before finding a local butcher. I've struck a deal with him for organic meat. We'll be eating a lot better before you know it." She placed some vegetable slaw, chicken, and potato salad onto his desk. Nick loved her cooking and wasn't going to complain.

Dean had also tasted her food and hated him for getting her raw talent.

"I've also baked a chocolate cake to keep you going until the end of the day."

He stared at the beauty before him.

"What else did you do, or is that it, food shopping?"

"I like food shopping. I cut some roses out of the garden for the table. I thought the house was looking a little bland and decided to add a splash of color." She did him a plate then herself one.

Nick kept his gaze on her. She was so sweet. Thinking about his need to claim her, he opened his mouth about to talk when a knock sounded on his door. His personal assistant would have buzzed him if it had been her.

Irritated that he'd been interrupted before he began, he got to his feet toward the door. He unlocked and opened it, seeing Dean looking concerned. "What is it?" Nick asked.

Dean looked into the room seeing Clara. "You need to get rid of her."

"What? Why?"

"The collective of alphas are here. Mark has been arrested along with many of the men selling women for money. Shit is about to hit the fan."

Clara was already cleaning away their lunch. Cursing, he watched her pack everything as the men of the collective alphas walked off the elevator. He counted five men. They were not all there. In fact, he saw at least one missing. Riley was the name, the one who had forced the issue of Nick's outlawed status.

"Too late."

"Dean, I see you've already informed Nick of our visit."

Nick recognized the man who spoke as Charles, one of the oldest men of the group. He didn't look a day over forty, but Nick knew he was close to seventy years of age.

"What warning? Dean was arranging to come to my house for dinner tonight. Clara's an amazing cook, and he is always looking for an excuse to visit." He gave Dean a pointed look, entering the office. Clara stood by his desk with a smile plastered to her face.

The five men entered his office as Dean took a seat.

"I'll see you at home tonight. I'll do my famous chicken curry," Clara said. She was nervous. Reaching out, he held her face, slamming his lips down on hers. Nick kissed the life out of her smelling her arousal when he was finished

"Baby, everything about you is famous."

"Who is this?" Charles asked.

"I'm his girlfriend. It's a pleasure to have met you all."

Clara made her excuses. Charles wasn't having any of it. "You're a female wolf who hasn't been outlawed. Why are you with Nick?"

She turned her gaze to his before looking back at the large man. He watched her tug her arm out of his hold.

"I'm in love with him. You have no right to insult him in his own building. Even the collective of alphas are not above showing respect." She turned back to him.

He saw the truth in her eyes. In front a room full of men who could take her away she'd told him she loved him.

"I'll see you tonight with only Dean?" she asked.

"You will, baby."

She left without another backward glance. Shit, he should have told her how he felt. Feeling like a bastard, he pushed it aside and concentrated on why the collective of alphas were in his office.

****

Great, Nick was probably laughing at her right now. Clara walked down the street swinging her basket from side to side. She'd made a complete fool of herself admitting her feelings. The moment Charles touched her, she'd sensed his power. There was a reason why the collective of alphas were needed. They were far stronger than all wolves.

She walked through the city park basking in the sunlight. Her body was still alive from their harsh fucking in his office.

Running fingers through her hair, she took one last look around the city before going home. The large house no longer looked dominating. Every day that passed she added a little touch of her own. Letting herself inside, she went straight to the kitchen to put the slaw and potato salad in the fridge. She'd not been kidding about the curry. The chicken was marinating in the fridge in plenty of spices.

Once everything was put away, she took a shower leaving her dress in the bedroom to make her way downstairs to the pool. For the next hour she tried to collect her thoughts as she took a long swim. Why was the collection of alpha in the offices?

Dean's words had been muffled. What did they want with Nick?

She'd seen the tension in Nick's whole body. Being honest in the room had been essential.

When she could put it off no longer, she went back to wash the pool from her body, changed into another summer dress, then went into the kitchen. She started making her curry, humming as the process soothed her.

Clara tensed when she heard the door open. Dean and Nick talking invaded her calmness.

Seconds later Nick entered the room. He looked tired, worn out.

"Did you mean what you said in my office?"

She dropped her head, not wanting to meet his gaze.

"Don't do that," he said. "Look at me and tell me the truth."

"Yes, I meant every word I said. I've fallen in love with you. I tried not to, and it's insane. I've not known you all that long, but I know how I feel and I love you." She pressed a hand to her lips, wishing the ground would open up and stop her from talking.

"For fuck's sake, Nick, go to her and tell her how you feel," Dean said. He was leaning against the doorframe watching them. She'd been so concerned about Nick she hadn't heard him enter.

"Get out of here. Go to the dining room or something, but give us some much needed privacy," Nick said, glaring at his friend.

Dean held his hands up. "I'm just trying to help a friend out. Don't let him get away with shit, Clara." He winked at her before leaving.

"Blasted man doesn't know when to stay out of other people's business."

"He cares about you." She picked up her wooden spoon to start stirring the sauce.

"The first night you were here I sneaked into your room," he said, taking her completely by surprise.

"What?"

"I saw you taking a shower. I left you my shirt, but when you were asleep I came back. We slept together that night. I held you in my arms leaving you before you woke."

"Your scent wasn't only on the shirt?"

"No, I was there all night."

"Why are you sharing all this with me?" she asked.

"You have a right to know. I shouldn't have kept you in the dark, but I did. The first day I took you, I was ready to mate with you, but I held myself back out of fear. I didn't want you to be afraid of me. I've wanted to mate with you for a while now, Clara." He held his hand up stopping her from talking when she would have. "I don't just want to mate with you because you're the only available female wolf to me. I love you, Clara."

His words lifted her spirits.

"Why are you telling me this?" she asked.

"I need you to know how I feel. I love you. It has nothing to do with the money I spent on you. I'd pay your parents again, over and over, to make sure I got you. You're amazing." He stopped, taking a step closer to her.

"Pussy." She heard Dean calling out the name.

Nick shot the door a glare but didn't back down.

"In the next couple of days you're going to get a visit from the collective of alphas."

She jerked back, worried. "What? Why?"

"They're hunting men and women who sell females to be used. Your father has been caught, and he's exposed me."

Clara reached out, pressing a hand to his chest.

"What are they going to do?"

"Your father and your family are being punished by the collective. They can't do anything to me as I'm outlawed already. I'm not bound by pack law, but your family broke the law. They're coming to see you, and it will be up to you what you want to do."

"What do you mean?"

He cupped her cheek, holding her close. "If you wish to leave to join your pack, you may do so. They'll take care of you giving you a home."

"Do you want me to go?" Only a minute ago he'd been telling her how much he loved her, and now he was telling her this. Clara felt torn in two on what to think.

Nick held her face, staring into her eyes. She saw the pain in his dark brown depths. "No, I don't want you to go, but I don't want you to feel forced to stay here. I love you, Clara. I want to mate with you. This is a choice you're going to have to make." He kissed her lips, pulling away. "The curry smells amazing. I need to run," he said, turning toward the door.

Unable to stop him, she watched him tear his clothes off and change within the next second.

"He's scared," Dean said, bringing her attention back into the room.

"Scared? Scared of what?" She was confused, and she hated the feeling.

"Nick is outlawed, and he bought you. I know you didn't have the best start in this relationship." Dean leaned over the kitchen counter. "If the collective choose to, they can take you away."

"What? Why?"

"You're a female who has been taken by an outlawed male. They could override your decision to stay with him. Their argument is accusing you of suffering with Stockholm syndrome."

"They're insane. I don't suffer with anything." She ran fingers through her hair, panicking. For the first time in her life, she was in love, and it could all be torn away from her.

"Do you care about what happens to your family?"

"No, I couldn't give a shit about what happens to them. They were not my family. They spent their whole life making me aware of how awful I was to their reputation." She let Dean see her anger.

"Look, you prove to the collective of your feelings about your family and your love for Nick and you can win. They wouldn't be able to take you away, but you also need to make a choice," Dean said.

"Choice, what choice?"

"If you ever want to be part of a pack again or not. Nick will never be held in their grip. He possesses the dangerous mark whereas you do not. Another pack will accept you with open arms."

Dean raised a brow, opening his hands.

Clara went back to her curry, hearing the pain of Nick's howl in the distance.

Chapter Twelve

Nick saw his friend out trying his best to ignore the sympathy in his eyes. Whatever happened was up to Clara. He wouldn't try to influence her decision. If the alphas found her suffering from some syndrome or another, he'd lose her either way. How had a simple business transaction turned into something so painful? He was in love with her. The thought of losing her left a giant hole inside his chest.

Clawing out his heart wouldn't be half as painful even if he would be dead. Clara was upstairs in their bedroom. She rarely spoke over dinner leaving him and Dean to talk business. He was tired of business and the incessant need to earn money. What was the point of earning money when he had no one to share it with?

Staring at his reflection in the mirror Nick let out a breath feeling the weight of the world on his shoulders. He'd been a good alpha, and he hoped to be a good mate.

"Nick?"

He turned to see the love of his life standing in the doorway. She wore a sheer white negligee that covered her body without really hiding her curves. He saw the hardness of her nipples pressing against the fabric along with the thatch of red curls between her thighs.

"I thought you'd gone to bed."

"I'm not going to bed without you." She took a step into the room.

Nick didn't move and watched her get closer, her hips moving seductively with every step she took.

She pressed her palms onto his chest. Taking hold of her hands, he tried to push her away.

"Don't!" She shouted the word, glaring at him. "They may have come into your office at lunchtime, but they're not here. Do not push me away."

"They could take you away from me. Do you really think I can handle making love to you knowing they're going to take you from me? It's killing me."

She shoved him hard, slapping his chest. "You selfish bastard." The anger on her face was clear. "Do you think I wanted this? For so long I was the fucking fat wolf of the pack. No one wanted me. I was humiliated on my eighteenth. No one wanted to be with me." She slapped a palm to her own chest. "Then just as suddenly I'm sold to a man I do not know, an outlawed man accused of murder, and I fall in love with him. You awaken my fucking body like it was your own."

He saw the pain in her eyes as they mirrored his own.

"I really thought I was happy to never have to worry about falling in love or being with a man. I gave you my virginity, Nick. I've given you a part of me. I don't care what happens to my family. They were never here with me. You were, and I will make sure they all know how I feel. I can live without a pack, but I can never live without you."

Unable to deny himself the pleasure of touching her, he gripped her neck, tugging her close. She wrapped her arms around him, holding him tightly. For many minutes they simply held onto each other, gaining comfort. He inhaled her sweet scent mixed with his own.

"I love you," she said. "Don't stop fighting. I won't."

Her hands ran up and down his chest. Nick watched her movements without pushing her away. Their future was in her hands when the alphas came to take her away.

"I love you, too, baby." He kissed her head. Staying still he waited for her to release the buttons of his shirt. She pushed the fabric from his shoulders. "This is all for you. You're the one in charge."

"Are you sure you trust me?" she asked, raising a brow.

He unbuckled his belt as she sank to her knees. Neither of them said another word as she peeled his trousers down his thigh, taking his boxer briefs with them.

His cock sprang free. The vein was thick along the side pulsing blood to his shaft. The tip already leaked his pre-cum. She gripped the base of his shaft, working from root to tip then back again.

Holding himself still, he watched her open her lips and take him in deep. Her tongue circled the tip, taking his cum from him.

It took every ounce of restraint not to force his cock all the way into her mouth. Clara set the pace, sucking on the tip then taking him an inch at a time. He stroked her hair, sinking his fingers into the length for something to hold on to.

Her gaze travelled up his body. When their gazes met she went down on him, taking him all the way until he hit the back of her throat. She sucked tightly, making him gasp. Up she went, circling the head before sliding down.

Over and over she sucked, licked and nibbled on his shaft. With her free hand, she fingered his balls. Nick closed his eyes grunting at the pleasure.

She moaned with his cock in her mouth, and the vibration sent another wave of pleasure inside him.

"No, I can't wait." Tugging her mouth off him with the grip on her hair, he threw the contents of his desk to the floor. Nick was crazed, not wanting to wait to get upstairs to claim her pussy. He placed her on the hard surface, gripping her hips as he guided his dick to her cunt. Clara gripped the edge of the desk.

"I love you," he said, feeling impassioned. Tonight, tomorrow, however long he had before the collective of alphas tried to take her away, he was going to fuck her, make love to her and prove to Clara with his actions how much he loved her.

"I love you, too."

Sliding his dick through her creamy cunt, he found her entrance and slammed in deep. Clara cried out, scoring his back as he took her over the edge. He was mindless with pleasure and with need.

Her pussy rippled around his shaft, gripping him tighter than any fist. Pulling out, he slammed back inside, going deeper. Clara's tits bounced with the jerk of her hips as he plunged deep into her.

"So fucking tight and sweet. I'm going to spend the rest of my life fucking you. Making love to you."

Nick didn't let up in his strokes. When she tightened around him, he made her finger her sweet pussy. Each stroke over her swollen clit sent her pussy squeezing him.

"That's it, baby. I'll give you my cum as soon as you give me yours."

"I love you, Nick."

"I know, baby. Give me what I need."

She stroked her nub, and seconds later she climaxed. Even as she was caressing her clit, Nick fucked her hard. The desk moved under the force of his thrusts. He didn't care. Finding his release was all he cared about. Plunging inside her, Nick stared into her eyes. She was so fucking beautiful. He'd die a happy man being inside her.

The stirrings started, and he plundered her tight heat spilling his cum into her waiting pussy. She took every drop, moaning as he held her tightly.

No one was taking her away from him. Nick would kill every last one of them if they even thought to take her from him.

****

Later that night, Clara padded back to the bedroom. She had brushed her teeth and washed her face. The whole of the night had been spent with Nick inside her. Clara's pussy was sore, but she didn't care. The feel of Nick's hard cock inside her was more than worth it.

"Your breath smelled fine to me."

She rolled her eyes and climbed on the bed beside him. Before brushing her teeth she'd been sucking his cock until he came, swallowing down every drop.

"I wanted to brush my teeth."

He reached out, tucking strands of hair behind her ear. "You're going to be the death of me."

Glancing down at his stiffening cock, she chuckled. "No, you're going to be the death of me. I've not even made it to the kitchen yet without you pouncing on me."

Nick caressed her ass, sliding his palm over her cheeks. "What can I say? You shouldn't be so fucking tempting."

He moved over her, trapping her legs together as he kissed and nibbled on her ass. She cried out as his teeth sank into her flesh. Moaning, she held onto the blanket as pleasure consumed her thoughts. Her cream leaked out, coating her clit.

The scent of their combined releases surrounded them.

"I could spend all day worshipping this ass," he said, slapping her cheek. She squealed at the slight pain then groaned at the pleasure. His fingers slid between her thighs, stroking her clit. The instant contact to her clit had her jerking up.

"Shh, baby. I'm going to make you feel so good." Two fingers plunged inside her pussy working her up into a frenzy.

"Please, Nick, fuck me." She was not above begging him to take her.

"I thought you didn't want me to fuck you anymore tonight?" he asked, teasing her.

"You better not leave me like this."

"I have no intention of leaving you wanting, but I think it's time to give your pussy a rest." Nick moved his fingers from between her thighs up to her ass. She tensed as he pressed against the tight puckered hole of her anus. "Relax, baby. I'm never going to hurt you."

Clara whimpered as he pressed his wet fingers to her ass.

"Relax, baby."

She slowly tried to relax her body for his penetration. His free hand caressed over her ass cheek then up her back soothing her.

"Give me what I want, and I'll make it feel fucking amazing."

Gripping the pillow, Clara took several breaths, relaxing her body for his invasion. Closing her eyes she allowed her body to feel rather than over-think what he was doing.

"Good girl. You're going to love me inside your ass. It gives you just that bite of pain you need to make it entirely pleasurable." He talked to her constantly as he pressed one finger into her ass. The bite of pain exploded within her. The pain soon turned to pleasure as he pumped his single finger in and out of her ass also tweaking her clit.

The combination of pleasure and pain had her thrusting back on his hand.

"Please, Nick," she said, not knowing what she

was begging for.

"I'm going to give you a second finger. Lift up to me," he said.

She went to her knees opening up for him.

"You want my cock in your hot little ass?" he asked.

"Yes."

Nick added a second finger, spreading her wider. He added more of their combined release to moisten her hole. Every single touch pushed her closer to the edge of her orgasm.

Moments later, he moved behind her, replacing his fingers with the tip of his large wide cock.

She whimpered as Nick caressed her back.

"You're going to love this, Clara. Trust me."

Not only did she trust him, she was in love with him. She knew deep in her heart Nick wouldn't do anything to harm her.

Staying still, she cried out as the head of him pushed past the tight ring of muscles, opening up her ass for his cock. His hands went to her hips, holding her in place. She laid her head flat on the bed, trying to focus on anything else but the pleasure along with the pain of his claiming.

Nick was a pro when it came to his cock. He knew what to do and how to draw the most pleasure out of her body.

In the bedroom alone he reminded her of many of the heroes she read about in the books she loved so much.

"I'm in, baby. Can you take more of me?" he asked.

"Yes."

The pain didn't take long to turn into mind-blowing pleasure. Slowly, he worked the rest of his cock inside her. She whimpered at how much he filled her.

With his cock in her ass she felt every pulse and jerk of his shaft. There was nothing to escape from. The last inch he slammed inside her, going as deep as he could.

She cried out, gripping the blanket tighter.

"This is where the real fun begins," he said, running his hands up and down her body.

"It can get better?"

"Much better." He worked her ass taking his time with each thrust.

Clara soon started to thrust onto his cock. There was no longer any pain, only mind-blowing ecstasy. She didn't want him to stop. Her body was on fire for his cock. The need built with every second.

"You love my cock in your ass?" he asked.

"Yes." No other words were needed. Their grunts echoed around the room along with the sound of flesh hitting flesh.

"Please, Nick."

"Do you need to come?"

"Yes."

"Then play with your pussy. Let me feel you come, baby."

She stroked her clit, whimpering at the merest touch. Three strokes over her nub had her screaming out her release.

"Fuck, that's it. Come all over my cock."

He fucked her hard, and Clara loved it. When he grunted she felt the pulse of his cock along with the heat of his cum. The sensation was entirely different from having him in her pussy.

"I think you've killed me," he said, slumping over her body with his cock still inside her.

"This is all you." She smiled loving his touch.

"I know. Come on, baby. It's time for you to have a bath."

Nick carried her into the bathroom. For the remainder of the night he took care of her, washing her body and providing her with every care possible.

Lying in his arms early the next morning after only an hour of sleep, Clara wondered if he was trying to get her out of his system. The collective of alphas could take her away, but she knew she wouldn't let it happen. Nick was the love of her life, and she wasn't going to let anyone take him away from her.

Chapter Thirteen

Three days later Nick was staring at his computer screen. Clara was at home after a marathon of sex. She was probably happy with the reprieve. His nerves were totally fried at what their future was going to be. Whatever happened was up to her.

He tried to focus on his work rather than on what his woman was going to do. The last three days he'd held back claiming her. The mating heat had been between them during most of their fuck fest, but he held it back. Nick didn't want them to blame the mating or him for Clara staying with him.

In the space of one month he'd found his woman, hurt her, taken her, fallen in love with her, and was now on the verge of losing her. His parents were not lying when they said wolves moved fast, refusing to waste a single moment of life.

Leaning back, he turned his chair to look over city life. When he was first outlawed he hated the city, but then he had come to love it. The hustle and bustle of activity stopped him from thinking about the pain of everything he lost. Looking over the city he couldn't stop feeling the pain of what he faced later today.

The door of his office opening forced him to turn. He saw Charles, one of the leaders of the collective of alphas.

"Have you gone to see her yet?" Nick asked. When he woke up this morning he felt today was the day they'd come for her.

"No, we're getting ready to go and see her. The other alphas are waiting for me downstairs." Charles closed the door, striding forward to take a seat in front of him.

"Why have you come to see me?" Nick shuffled

some files, trying to keep himself busy. This man had never terrified him in all the years of being an alpha for a pack. Now, he felt real fear. The power Charles had made Nick sick to his stomach.

"I wanted to come and see you. I'm sure you're aware we're stopping the auctioning and selling of females wolves?"

"Yes, I'm aware of it. Dean keeps me in the know of wolf business."

"I know. I'm the one who tells him what to say," Charles said.

Nick stayed silent for several minutes hoping the man would end his misery.

"Why are you here?" he asked, when the other man made no move to say why he'd come back to see him.

"I'm disgusted with myself. From what I've learned many women have been sold behind the collective's back, by one of us. It makes us all feel old when one of our own can pull the wool over our eyes." Charles let out a sigh. "Your woman is one of the women who was sold, right?"

Taking in a breath, Nick locked his fingers together resting his hands on the desk. "I wanted a female wolf to fuck. I was made aware of being able to purchase a woman. I paid over a million dollars for Clara. She was the runt, an outcast of her pack. Her mother and father, along with all of her family, treated her appallingly."

"You used her for sex?" Charles asked.

"When I first bought her it started out as sex. I didn't want or need anything else."

"Something changed?"

Nick paused, thinking about the change of his feelings over the last few weeks. "Yes, everything changed. I no longer wanted to just fuck Clara. She came to mean something to me. The first night in my home I held her while she slept. Holding her gives me as much pleasure as watching her read." Nick stopped, remembering her lying on the sofa in his office reading as he worked. "She's beautiful inside and out. Her family didn't deserve her."

"And you do?"

He looked at Charles, weighing up his answer.

"No, I don't deserve her. She's better than I ever will be. I've never been a good man. I thought I was a good alpha at one point, but I wasn't. If I was a good alpha, I wouldn't have been outlawed. Clara makes me a better man, and I know I'm going to spend the rest of my life showing her how much I love her."

Charles stayed quiet for a long time.

"The decision to outlaw you was taken out of my hands. I didn't disagree with what you did. The fact I sat at the same table with that man, ate with him, shared my life with him sickens me. I saw the damage he did. You were outlawed because one of us was determined to see you out of the way. Riley has a lot to answer for. He was the cause for the sale of women. He wanted you outlawed so everyone would tell your story rather than realize what he was doing. He made us believe we were doing the right thing, and for that, I'm totally sorry." Charles stood. "You were one of the best alphas we've ever known. Our biggest regret is outlawing you."

"Riley did this?" Nick asked, understanding why the other collective alpha hadn't made an appearance.

"Yes. We found out what he was doing, and we're stopping him. I know words are not enough, but I am sorry for not going with my gut and leaving you as an alpha."

Nick was thankful for the words even though they

were unnecessary.

"If you were given the option of having a pack would you take it?" Charles asked.

"No, I don't want the responsibility. The only person I want is Clara."

"Speaking of the wonderful woman, I better go and join the rest of the collective to interview her."

Nick watched the other man walk toward the door. "Wait," he said, halting him. Charles turned. "When you're with her take your time. She doesn't trust people easily, and I'd hate for you to upset her."

"I will take every effort to calm her."

Charles left, and Nick slumped back into his seat. There, his life was going to be over if they decided Clara didn't know her own mind. Closing his eyes, he listened to his employees walking into the building. He hated them all for their happy easy lives.

Getting on with work he kept looking at his phone waiting for it to ring. It didn't ring at all.

Around lunchtime he tensed as Dean entered the office. The somber look on his face didn't help Nick's nerves at all.

"Do you know anything?" Nick asked.

"Sorry, mate, no. I brought you the contract we agreed to. It's time for you to look over it before you sign." Dean placed the file on the table. "You've not heard anything?"

"No. I've heard fuck all. This shouldn't be allowed to happen. I feel like my life is on hold until I know what is happening."

"Clara's a strong woman, Nick. She'll convince them. I know she's in love with you. She's not going anywhere."

He smiled at his friend, not believing a word.
****

Clara kept beating the butter and sugar together. She looked at the time sensing something was going to happen today. Nick had held her tighter than ever before. Seeing him drive away clearly sad had upset her even more. Today was going to be the day they visited her. The collective's visit was the only explanation as to Nick's change in mood.

Baking a dark rich chocolate cake usually eased her thoughts. Her cure for all tensions was no longer working. She placed the two filled cake tins in the oven, washing up the dishes. Clara was wiping down the counter when the doorbell sounded. Glancing around the kitchen, she tried to find any excuse to answer the damn thing.

Be strong, Clara. You can do this.

She loved Nick, and all she needed to do was prove to them her feelings. Tucking hair behind her ears she walked to the door.

"Hello, Clara. I'm Charles, and these are my brothers. I'll be the one doing the talking today. They're here to listen, learn, and take information in," Charles said, going over all the introductions.

"Can I tell you to fuck off?" she asked.

"You can, but we can't go anywhere. These are the rules."

Nodding, she opened the door waiting for them all to enter. She heard them scenting the air. "I've been doing some baking. Would you please sit in here while I get the tea?" Clara ushered them into the sitting room like they were a pack a sheep rather than hungry dogs waiting to take her away.

Once they were seated, she went into the kitchen, tempted to call Nick. No, she wouldn't do something to make them believe she wasn't here of her own free will. She took the cakes out of the oven to cool, making up the tray with six cups and sugar.

Entering the sitting room, she placed the tray on the coffee table remembering her and Nick's time together. Heat entered her core. She ignored the need, serving them all a drink and taking a seat even as her arousal increased.

"Why are you aroused?" Charles asked.

Her cheeks must be aflame at his obvious question. "I'm remembering a time with Nick, in this very room." Lifting the cup to her lips she took a sip smiling. "It's a good memory."

"Clara, we must get down to business. I'm sure you know why I'm here?"

"I've been told you're to make sure I don't suffer with some kind of syndrome and that I'm here of my own free will." She was speaking too fast, but she couldn't stop the words from pouring out. Sipping her tea she cursed her wayward mouth with her constantly trying to talk.

Shut up, Clara. Be confident. You're not lying. You're telling the truth.

For the next hour Charles took over the conversation asking her questions. He asked about her childhood up to her first turning. The look on his face as she described what happened made her feel slightly scared. There was a reason these men were the collective. They knew how to handle wolves and were stronger than many other wolves.

I bet Nick can take you.

He started asking questions about the night of her being taken, becoming Nick's property. She answered all of the questions truthfully. There was no need for her to lie about her feelings. She had hated Nick on sight, but she made sure all of them knew he didn't lay a finger on her.

When it got to the intimacy between her and Nick she looked down at her lap thinking about their time together. Arousal filled her core at the feel of Nick touching her.

"From the moment he bought me he could have touched me, hurt me." She felt tears fill her eyes. "He was the perfect gentleman. I mean, I hated him, but he was so nice. You hear such horrid stories of being sold for sex, yet I was lucky. Nick is not a man to be thwarted. He never raised a hand to me in anger. Every single time we were together he was sweet, coarse at times, but I never felt scared of him."

She rubbed her arms, wishing he was with her now, wrapping his arms around her to protect her. Clara said as much to them.

"Your family has been punished and is sentenced to over fifty years of hard labor in our jail cells. They will never come near you again or hurt you. Nick will never become an alpha of a pack. I need to know if you wish to go back to a pack," Charles said.

"No, I don't want to be part of a pack. Nick is everything I need. I know not all packs are horrible. I've had more than my fair share of being part of a pack. I'd rather be outlawed with him," she said, pouring him another cup of tea.

Charles nodded, stared at her for several moments and turned to the silent men in the room.

"I believe we've gotten everything we need."

The other men nodded, rose to their feet and said their goodbyes. She watched them leave, silently. Charles remained, sipping his tea.

"What's going on? You're not taking me away, are you?" Clara asked, ready to fight him.

"No, we're not going to take you away. Regardless of our reputation we're not some horrid beasts separating people for fun." Charles was smiling as he spoke. "I see you love Nick and his love of you. I visited him this morning before coming here today."

"You did? Was he okay? I'm so worried about him." She stopped, biting her lip at her questions.

Charles chuckled. "Nick is an alpha. I know it took a lot out of him to leave you alone to deal with us. It has been a pleasure seeing him happy."

"He told me what happened to make him an outlawed male," Clara said, heart breaking for the man she loved.

"Yes, it was nasty business but had to be done. My biggest regret in being a collective is outlawing Nick. I'm pleased to see he has fallen for a woman who makes him happy."

"Do you really think I make him happy?" she asked, looking up at the man as he started to get to his feet.

"Yes, you're Nick's life mate. You're both attuned to each other. Your emotions are the same. Together, I know you will flourish."

Clara got to her feet to see him out.

When they were at the door she stopped him with a hand on his arm. "What would you have done if I wanted to leave?" she asked.

"I'd have taken you away today to a new pack. Every month I would have visited to make sure you were settled." Charles cupped her cheek. "I'm not going to tear you away from your mate. Have a happy life, Clara."

He left afterward. Looking at the clock she saw she'd missed lunch. Nick was probably out of his mind. Rushing to the phone she started to type in his number and stopped. Calling him wouldn't do the trick. She wanted to do something else. Putting the phone down, she entered the kitchen and started setting up her basket.

Nick deserved the best, and she finished icing the chocolate cake. She hummed as she set to work. By the time it came to end of the day, she headed out toward Nick's place of work. At five o'clock she was leaning against his car holding the picnic basket in front of her. Every time the elevator stopped, she tensed waiting to see him.

For the next half an hour Nick didn't appear. He was one of the last men to leave the building coming toward her with Dean in tow. His friend slapped his arm, pointing at the car.

She smiled, waving at him. Nick frowned, approaching her.

"Why are you here?" Nick asked.

"I thought we could go on a picnic. I've packed dinner." She turned to Dean, smiling at him, hoping he'd get the message and leave.

Dean said his goodbyes leaving them alone.

"Did you see the collective today?"

"Yes, I saw them, and I'm here."

"You're not leaving?" Nick asked.

Tears filled her eyes as his spilled down his cheeks. She'd never seen Nick cry before. The emotion coming off him made her gasp.

"No, I'm not going anywhere." His arms wrapped around her making the picnic basket collapse to the floor.

She giggled, holding onto him as they shared a tender moment.

"I'm not going anywhere. I'm afraid you've got me for the rest of your life," Clara said.

"I don't care. Fuck, marry me, Clara," he said.

"Yes." She didn't even hesitate, kissing his lips as his love surrounded her. He held her tightly, neither of them wanting to let go.

"You've made me the happiest man in the

world," he said.

Clara couldn't speak. Who would have thought being bought for sex could have resulted in her finding the man of her dreams? Nick was her life mate, the man she was destined to spend the rest of her life with.

Taking his hand, she led him out to the park to celebrate their newfound freedom.

Epilogue

Five years later

Nick stared down into his mate's eyes. This was their fifth anniversary of being a mated couple. Dean, godfather to their six children, all twins, had taken them for the night so Nick could show his woman how much he loved her.

"You're tormenting me again," she said, whimpering.

He turned her over, dripping some cream onto her back and licking up the droplets. Pressing the strawberry to her lips he watched the plumpness take the fruit.

"We don't get much time alone anymore. We've got to take as much time as we can." It had taken him over three weeks to get Dean to agree to take their kids. In all fairness all three sets of twins were not the easiest children to look after. Nick adored them, but he was pleased for them to be out of the house so he could have some quiet time with his wife.

After convincing the collective that she loved him, Clara had accepted his marriage proposal and that very same night he gave her his mating mark. Any wolf would see she was mated and how possessive he'd been in the claiming of her.

"Then you better stop feeding me and fucking me. Oh, before you do," she said, getting up and pushing him to his back. Nick laughed loving how wild she was when the kids were away. Clara really was an amazing mother. Their children were always around her feet. When he went to pick the oldest up from school he heard the mothers commenting on how wonderful she was.

He knew how amazing she was. Nick had been the one to pick her. She'd been his virgin possession, and he was determined to make her feel loved.

"What could you possibly have to tell me?" he asked, loving her curves.

"Do you love me?" she asked, kissing down his chest.

"You know I do." He moaned as she sucked the tip of his cock into her mouth.

"Are you sure?"

"Yes, dammit." Fuck, he was going to explode.

She pulled off his shaft. "I'm pregnant again." Her smile was bright as she tried to hold in her laughter.

"Fuck me. When can I fuck you without knocking you up?" he asked, grabbing her and pinning her to the bed.

He slid inside her, watching the pleasure cross her face.

"I don't know, baby, at least we know I'm not going to get pregnant now."

Nick moaned, making love to her. He really did love his wife.

Nine months later, he welcomed another set of twins. Kissing his wife, Nick started thinking about looking for a bigger house.

The End

SAM CRESCENT

THE ALPHA'S DOMINATION

The Alpha Shifter Collection, 4

Sam Crescent

Copyright © 2014

Chapter One

Daniel Brennan ran through the forest inhaling all the delicious scents and listening to all the sounds that surrounded him during a run. He needed to clear his head before he headed toward his BDSM club. Some of his pack was following him, being the loyal guards they craved to be, while others were at the club. None of his pack lived with him. He'd never been one of those Alphas who demanded the pack's presence at all times. They were free to roam within his area, and the only rule he demanded they all follow was that the secret of the wolf be kept at all times. Obviously, if one of the men or women were to find their mate, he wouldn't mind that secret being divulged. Serious shit happened between mated couples, and secrets were easily kept.

He rounded the forest and took off at a run with the others following behind him. Being the Alpha of the pack made him faster and stronger than anyone else. Daniel loved the power even though he never used it against any member. He'd never been into cruelty or demeaning others. They were his pack, and he loved them like he would his children. Daniel had heard of other packs where cruelty occurred, but he'd yet to meet any of them.

Once he ran off the burst of energy, he stood looking over his property. His family came from old money, and so his house was large, big enough to contain a pack.

"Okay, you're fast, we get that," Jake said, taking several deep breaths. "Shit, did you have to prove to us how great and powerful you are?"

Chuckling, Daniel glanced at his friend, who also happened to be one of the guards who assigned himself to taking care of him. "You're the one, along with Dave and Bill, who sticks around to protect me. I don't need protecting, Jake."

"We all know this, and none of us care what you say. We're going to stick beside you no matter what."

Daniel rolled his eyes. He wasn't being a pain in the ass and truly believed he didn't need help protecting himself. In all the years he'd been alpha he'd not once had any conflict with any outsiders. Any pack that entered his territory presented themselves and requested permission to stay within his area for a few days or weeks. Not once had he encountered a rogue wolf or someone of any threat. They were all peaceful, and he worked with them to ease life for his pack. He heard of other Alphas who did nothing but fight, argue, and cause problems trying to overtake other territories.

"Are you going to see *her*?" Jake asked.

The smile on Daniel's face disappeared. The *her* being his very stubborn, pain in the ass mate who didn't acknowledge him as a mate or anything other than a Master.

"I'm going to see her. I've got no choice." He gritted his teeth, fisting his hands as the anger and longing combined together. Daniel couldn't have the woman he wanted as she held herself away from him.

"You're going to Kinkster's then?"

He nodded. Kinkster's was the local BDSM club that he helped to run. They catered to the wolves with a taste for the rougher, kinkier side of sex. Some of the members were human as mates were not restricted to their own kind. Daniel didn't mind. He wasn't against mates in whatever form they came in. The world, at times, was extremely cruel. For a wolf to find their one true mate was a gift that few enjoyed. Some men stopped looking for their mates and settled down with the next best thing. The only problem with settling down for the next best thing was when they finally stumbled upon the woman destined to be theirs.

"I've got no choice. She'll be there, and I know my wolf will not allow me to lose her because I hate what's going on between us." There was nothing going on. Dawn Weldon had entered his life one year ago and taken to screwing with his head. She didn't know how she screwed with him, but she was stubborn.

Dawn wasn't part of his pack, but, however, she'd approached him for permission to be allowed inside Kinkster's. She was a submissive inside, craving whatever his men could dish out, whether it be from a hand or a cane. The moment she entered his house he'd scented the need to mate, to claim, to possess. Those feelings only intensified while she'd been in his company dressed in a simple black pencil skirt and white blouse. The conservative clothes didn't repel him. He scented the darker cravings within her. The submissive wolf begged for some help, his help to tame the fire within. Not one word left her lips as they'd stared at each other, assessing, waiting.

He sensed her wolf, could see it as if she changed in front of him. The dark black wolf with hints of brown needed a strong hand, a firm hand. For the first time in his life, he'd sensed what true submission was all about, and Dawn had it all locked up in her dark skinned body. Her hazel eyes shot fire at him while her curvy body begged for him to take her and fuck her. Dawn was all woman with large tits, full rounded hips, and a curving stomach. To him, she would take a fucking without any fear of hurting her. Her legs were thick and strong as well. Her body was pure perfection, and always had him hard as rock. Even as her wolf wanted to lie down in submission, the woman in front of him put up a fight. Dawn and her wolf were together as one, but she was determined not to put her future in the hands of a person she didn't trust. For as much as she was submissive, she wasn't stupid either. Daniel respected her.

His mate didn't crave any kind of submission at the hands of a cruel man. She wanted to be submissive for the right man who'd take care of her and treat her right, not like some animal.

The scars inside her ran deep, and yet, she boxed them away as if there was not a care in the world. She wouldn't acknowledge his claiming. They'd never fucked, and he'd not met her pack alpha.

Her one and only request was that her presence remain a secret. She didn't want him to approach her pack alpha, and as her mate and Dom, he couldn't do what she asked him not to. With every day that passed he tried to prove to her over and over again that she could trust him.

She allowed him to touch her, but only in punishment never in intimacy.

Their relationship was pitiful, but it's what he needed. His wolf calmed a little when he was with her and now refused to lose that just because of her being difficult.

"You could find someone else, Daniel. You don't have to put up with this crap." Jake placed a hand on his shoulder.

"I've got no choice. She's my other half. My only reason for going to Kinkster's now." From the moment Dawn entered his life, she'd destroyed him for any other woman. He used to take pleasure in training submissives and sharing a unique lifestyle with other women. Now, he depended on Dawn. She didn't have the first clue of the power she held over him. He saw it in her eyes when they were together. She didn't trust her responses or her senses. Had her senses let her down in the past? He didn't know. There was so much he didn't know about his woman. She was a mystery he wanted to solve.

"The rest of the pack, do they share your thoughts?" Daniel asked.

"They're concerned for their Alpha, their leader. You've got to understand their worries."

"I've got to understand nothing, Jake. I care for my pack, and no decision I make is easy." He ran a hand down his face feeling the desire to find his mate. His wolf wished to bask in her scent and to see her submission at his feet.

"We know you'll take care when you make this decision. We're just concerned about you. Your wolf has run every day for the last month. Nothing you do seems to lock him up tight. Dawn keeping you at arms'-length is driving your wolf hard. One year, Daniel, one year you've been going through this. Something needs to stop."

He turned to look at Jake. Dave and Bill were standing a good distance away, but he saw the tension in their bodies.

"You're worried I'm going to let my beast take over?" Daniel asked.

"Worse things have happened in the past."

Some women who deny their mates could sometimes set about the feral beast within. When the feral instinct hit, everyone was in danger.

"I'm not going to let it get that far. I've got a handle on everything. Dawn needs guidance and care. I'm not going to rush her just because my wolf demands more." If he rushed Dawn all the work they'd put in together on their relationship would be over. As much as he'd love to spread her open and fuck her from sunrise to sunset, he knew he craved more.

"We trust you," Jake said.

The look Dave and Bill sent him told him another story. They trusted him, but with Dawn they were starting to doubt his leadership.

It was time to put Dawn in the picture of what she was doing to him.

****

Twirling the straw in her glass, Dawn watched the liquid swirl around. She'd been sitting at the bar for the last hour. The sounds of feminine and masculine moans filled the air. Kinkster's wasn't like many BDSM clubs. The bar didn't sell liquor but cups of tea, coffee, espresso, or in her case, sodas. She loved drinking soda. The taste was so refreshing, reminding her a lot of her youth when life was easy, simple. Life had stopped being simple at her transition when her life had changed forever. Dawn held a secret that she couldn't tell anyone, not even her own father. She was wolf, through and through, and only her need to be controlled set her apart from others within her pack. Spinning around in her seat, she looked at the people before her. Some of the people were human mates while many of them were wolves. Her pack was in the territory three towns over, and she came to Kinkster's as none of them did. None of her pack ever believed in BDSM. She'd heard what they said when this club opened.

Running fingers through her hair, she watched a woman who was bent over a spanking bench get her ass tanned. Her tender white flesh blushed a nice rouge as the man, her Dom, went at her for some misdemeanor. The scene left Dawn's cunt creaming. Her skin was dark, and it took a lot for her ass to show any hint of red. She knew as she'd been told before. Finding a man to become her Master or Dom had put her in some bad situations. The men within her pack didn't believe in taking a hand or cane to woman, let alone punishing her. She wished she could say as much for one woman in the pack. Dawn closed her eyes as memories flooded her at what she'd done to herself. She'd gone out amongst the humans to find what she craved. Her fear and need had disguised the natural scent of the people around her.

The first man she allowed herself to be free with had tied her up for two days and whipped her body leaving blood trailing down to the floor. He'd been a sadist of the worst kind. While he'd been in his high of thinking he was hurting her, he let slip that he'd killed a woman because she couldn't handle his kind of punishment.

Her wolf hadn't liked that and had come out of her haze to kill him. She had turned her hands into claws and torn him apart. For a long time she'd stared at the mess she created of the man then took care of the evidence. He was scum, and no one missed him. After her first disaster in BDSM, she'd decided to leave it alone. Wanting pain, needing pain, and craving pain had to be pushed aside. The pain she craved that no matter what anyone did to her, she couldn't feel. She couldn't allow herself to become vulnerable to anyone. Wolves were not submissive and did not enjoy that bite of pain to get them off, nor did they hunt for someone to hurt them in the hope of feeling it. She didn't know why she was different from the others in her pack, but out of fear she didn't ask anyone what they experienced.

The couples she saw in the pack were always sweet together. Her first time had been awful, and the guy she'd shared it with had held her down as he rode her body hard. The only thing she recalled liking was being held down and the fact she couldn't feel anything as he bit her during his release. From that point her need to find pain had only grown. Her wolf knew what she wanted, and so did Dawn.

"I'm sorry, Master."

Dawn followed the sound to see a man embracing his submissive. He wore a pair of jeans, and that was all. His arms were around his woman, and he stroked her hair. "Next time you'll take care, won't you?" he asked.

Her curiosity got the better of her, and she found herself watching the couple. She didn't know their names or their relationship to each other. The scent coming off them told her they were both wolves.

"Tara didn't take any precautions while she was out shopping and walked in front of an oncoming bus. If Dale hadn't been close by, she'd have lost their unborn baby, and could have been killed. We can withstand a lot, but a head on collision with a bus is pushing it a bit," Daniel said, sitting beside her.

Fisting her hands on her knees, she tried to fight the need to look at him.

You're mates. Stop fighting it.

According to Daniel they were mates, but she didn't trust the feelings going through her body. She'd been in such awful predicaments that she didn't have the first clue what to believe anymore. Her wolf craved his harsh punishment as did she, yet they were both cautious, their past mistakes and cravings making them wary.

He stared at her. All his male perfection taunted her with what she could have and held herself away from. Was he here to mock her?

He'd never do that to you. Stop treating him like the others.

She forced herself to look at him and then wished she hadn't. Daniel wasn't wearing a shirt like most of the men in the club. However, when Daniel was semi-naked, she couldn't focus on anything but his revealed flesh. His usually pale skin was tanned from the hours he spent in the sun. The same skin was covered in different kinds of ink. None of the ink was colored or elaborate. The designs were in black ink, pretty simple, yet they stood out on his body, which was strong, thick, and muscular. He made her mouth water when she simply looked at him. She quickly glanced down at her skirt, wishing she'd put something more on. When Daniel stood beside her, he made her feel small, delicate. Her size sixteen curves next to him felt like nothing. He pulsed with energy and power. The Alpha wolf inside him exuded everything she wanted in a man and a leader.

Don't trust.

Her wolf's inner warnings made her tense up.

"Look at me, Dawn."

He spoke harshly. Her body awakened once again, and she looked at him. His black hair hung over his face brushing the tops of his eyes. Daniel didn't have a lot of hair, but he had enough of it that she was left wanting to run her fingers through it. His brown gaze was focused entirely on her. She shivered at the power, the slight hint of amber as his wolf came to the surface.

Mate.

"Thank you for telling me," she said. "Are they your wolves?"

"What's wrong?" he asked.

"Nothing. I was just curious about the couple." She offered a smile even though smiling was the last thing she wanted to do.

"You're lying to me again."

She bit her lip, glancing down at her hands.

Dawn released a gasp, and he picked her up off the stool she sat on and took her seat. In quick moves he had her sitting on his lap. The evidence of his erection pressed against her ass, mocking her.

This is what you could have but never will because you're a coward.

His hand settled on her leg. Daniel didn't push the boundaries she set. He was the perfect gentleman and Master.

"Tate and Dale have been coming to Kinkster's for five years. They're a truly happy mated couple."

"She's happy being a submissive?"

"They like to play, Dawn. Mated or not, they know what they like."

Dawn licked her lips as her nipples beaded at the sound of his voice. The heat of his body surrounded her, filling her with hope for something more. Her pussy was on fire for his touch. It had been a year since she last experienced an orgasm, maybe a little longer. Her last partner left when he couldn't give her what she wanted. He told her she needed to find someone willing to put up with her crap. She was always on the hunt to feel pain, a lot of it, and she liked being held down. Some men didn't like being in charge completely. That's all she wanted, a man to be in complete control and to give her pain. During her early years, she would have given anything to stop feeling pain. Now, she wanted the pain to know she was alive, that something wasn't missing.

Look what happened all the times we've let them.

She closed her eyes as all of her failed attempts played through her like a broken record. At the ripe age of twenty-nine, she'd killed one man and been hurt by six more in a relationship. Being told you were a sick, disgusting, or plain weird, hurt just as much as punch. Dawn didn't like being punched at least, or she didn't used to. Now, she didn't feel it. She liked being spanked, punished in the most delicious of ways as the touch was better than nothing.

"You can't go anywhere," Daniel said, capturing her chin and turning her to face him. The grip on her face was hard, and he didn't let go. "What did I tell you when you came here?"

"That I'm with you and I can't go anywhere else."

"That's right, pet. You came to me because you needed strong discipline and a harsh hand. You're trying to fight me, and I'm tired of it." He placed her on her feet and stood.

"What are you doing?"

Daniel shot her a glare.

"Sir? What are you doing, Sir?"

"We're going to deal with your punishment. Inside Kinkster's you're my submissive unless you say your safe word." He took hold of her hand leading her away from witnesses. Even as her heart raced in fear of what was to come, she couldn't help the hit of arousal. Seeing him in the zone of a Dom turned her on.

Chapter Two

Daniel passed several members of his pack who gave him a quick nod. He greeted them but kept moving as he did. Dawn kept by his side with her head bowed. She wasn't acting the part of the submissive; she was simply following him. He noticed through watching her that she kept her head down whenever she moved from place to place. Dawn rarely looked up to see the world around her. Her life hadn't been easy. He'd seen the evidence in her eyes as well as in her actions. She'd been hurt in the past.

He wanted to know all of her secrets and what she was hiding from him. Mates didn't hide the truth from each other. She responded to him the way a mate did, yet he felt her wolf tense around him. For a woman and her wolf to be unsure, he knew whatever happened had scarred both of them. It was up to him to draw her out.

Opening the final door at the end of the corridor, Daniel released her hand, turned the light on, and locked the door. He turned to face her to assess her reactions. This was his private room. The only time he used this room was for the woman he intended to keep. Only a couple of women had even come close to getting inside here until this woman requested permission to join the club.

"Where are we?" she asked.

She stayed away from the bed, keeping it to her back as she rounded to look at him.

"This is my personal, private room. From now on, you come to this club, we'll be here." He folded his arms, waiting for her.

"No, we need to be in view of others."

"In front of others you hold yourself back.

Outside you're not yourself, and you're always afraid of someone noticing you. I've seen the way you are. You want to watch what happens within the club to make sure the men and women are treating their submissives right, but when it comes to you, you want the freedom of being away from it all."

"No, you're wrong."

"Then remove your clothes and we'll go out and do a scene right now. I'll punish you for your lack of acknowledgement of authority, and then I'll bring you off for all to see the beauty of your orgasm."

She withdrew from him. Her body tightened, and she started to look around the room. For a chance to escape? The wolf inside her started to bang against her inner cage.

The protective instinct inside him rose to full force. Her reactions were setting the Dom and the protector off all at once.

"On your knees and present to me." He deepened his voice, and Dawn went to her knees, spreading her legs wide as she bowed her head, presenting her body in the submissive pose he loved so much. "Your wolf can rest. I wouldn't let you out there for others to see this gorgeous body." He reached out to finger a strand of her hair. She had beautiful hair, long and dark brown. He watched the strands as he stroked them through his fingers. "Things are going to change between us, Dawn."

She looked up at him. Tears glistened in her eyes as she stared back at him, and her lips trembled.

"For the last year I've watched you dance around me like you were in control. I'm the Dom, your Master, and I'm also your mate." He pressed a finger to her lips as she went to dispute him. "No more arguing. You've kept me at bay, and I've followed your rules. Shit happened to you, I get it, but you're not going to deal with it anymore. You're going to let me inside here." He pressed the finger from her mouth to her head. "I'm not backing down or going away. We're in this together." He waited for several minutes to pass. "You may speak."

"This is not what we agreed. When I saw you, you promised I could take my time getting used to you and that I could end this when I want."

"I agreed to those terms before I realized how damaged you'd become from this lifestyle. You've got problems, Dawn. I can help you through them, but you've got to trust me."

"How can I trust you when you're doing this?" She waved her hand between them.

Did she have any idea how beautiful she looked on her knees before him? He doubted it. Dawn didn't have the first clue of the power she held over him.

"I didn't go to your father when I realized you weren't going to accept our mating." Any father, especially an Alpha, would have loved for their daughter to mate with a fellow alpha. Daniel had had every intention of going to her father. She'd begged him not to then threatened to deny his claim. If she denied his claim the risk of going feral increased. He backed off and decided to prove to her that she could trust him.

"I gave you an ultimatum. That's not trust."

He cupped her face, running his finger along her lip. She didn't tense up or jerk away, which was an improvement. When they were first together she fought him at every turn and pulled away from any kind of intimacy.

"I've given you more in the last year than you've ever gotten elsewhere. I see the look in your eyes, Dawn. You don't allow me to bring you to orgasm, yet the pleasure is there in your eyes, the way you let me hold you. There's much you can accuse me of, but caring and seeing to your needs is not one of them." He withdrew his hand. "You've been through a lot of crap. I want to know what it is."

"No, I'm not telling you anything."

"You feel your wolf right now? How she's pacing along the walls of your mind, curious yet holding herself back?"

"How did you—"

"She wants to trust me, to trust this instinct inside her. You've put yourself in danger, and we're not going anywhere else until you tell me what." He stared at her knowing he needed to win this battle. "Tonight, you're coming home with me. We're going to get to the bottom of your problems. No one lies at my house. We'll be totally alone, and we can explore your issues."

"No, I'm not going anywhere with you."

"It's simple, Dawn, you'll come with me back home or I'll be escorting you home, telling your father, and withdrawing your membership here. No one will touch you, and your father will either cast you out or demand something of you."

"You can't do this. I'll reject you. I'll stop this."

"The whole of your club will know your secret. You keep it a secret here with me and it will die with me, but you'll come home with me. I've kept this secret for a year. I've put up with your shit, and it ends now." This was a radical move on his part. She could walk out that door and be safe for the rest of her life. Daniel knew there was something else wrong inside her. Dawn was terrified of her own instincts, which told him she'd put herself at risk in more ways than one.

"This isn't fair."

"Life's not fair. I will never harm you, Dawn. I'm your mate. I'll take care of you, and I promise you everything that happens will be what you want."

She looked at a point past his shoulder. Her lips opened then closed. He imagined her mind working on overdrive to get out of his suggestion. "I don't want you telling my father anything. He doesn't need to know where I spend my time."

"Fine," he said, hurt that she was embarrassed by the way she spent her time.

Her nails sank into the flesh of her thighs, he imagined causing a bite of pain. He didn't like what she was doing. Going to his knees he took hold of her hands to stop her from causing herself more pain. She gasped at his touch, and he didn't look away from her eyes. "What's it going to be, Dawn? This can't go on."

"We're mated?"

"Yes."

She broke their gaze by looking at his hand holding her. "What do you need me to do?"

"I need you to trust me."

"I'm not normal."

"I've never said I wanted normal, pet. We're going to get through this."

He squeezed her hand in an attempt to reassure her. She let out a breath.

"Okay, I'll come with you."

Daniel wished there was more enthusiasm in her voice, but he'd take what she gave him right now. Mating was different for everyone. There were couples who were able to fight the impulse to mate, but that was usually down to the fact one of them were already in a relationship with someone else. In their case, his and Dawn's, she'd been hurt in the past, and she didn't trust the natural instinct to mate. When they did finally mate, there would be no way to deny each other. Once Dawn accepted him and he fucked and bit her, she'd be his, and their connection would be complete. He would understand everything that went on inside her head. If it wasn't for Jake, he wouldn't have known Dawn was the daughter of an alpha. His friend found out everything. It was one of the reasons it made him a good guard to have. Nothing ever got past him.

****

What are you doing?

Dawn stared at his hand where he held her palm inside his. Her dark flesh stood out in contrast to his pale skin, but their different skin colors didn't bother her. No, what struck her was the way he held her. He was strong, powerful, and yet he held her as if she was delicate. She was anything but delicate. He didn't hurt her, simply held her steady.

What was he trying to do?

"Look at me, Dawn."

She lifted her gaze to his, confused by what was happening inside her. On the one hand she wanted to continue sinking her fingers into her flesh to try to cause pain, and yet, she wanted what Daniel gave her. Would he even understand what was happening to her?

"You've been disobedient to me today. Before we go to my house you're going to get punished and then you're going to call your father."

When she went to speak, he pressed a finger to her lips to stop her. "No, you don't get to speak right now. I won't be leaving you alone. You're going to take the call while I'm here to listen to what you've got to say. I'll not have an angry father thinking I've stolen his daughter."

She hadn't even thought of starting a conflict between Daniel and her father. Dawn was many things, but a starter of fights wasn't one of them. The thought of having one or two men fighting over her turned her stomach.

"I wouldn't do that," she said.

Dawn would accept any punishment Daniel felt he needed to dish out. She'd been pushing him for the last year, and he had a right to punish her.

You like his punishments.

She didn't care what he used—hand, cane, whip, or paddle, she loved it all. Daniel was inventive with the restrictions she'd given him.

"You wouldn't? Some women would do anything to create a war between two territories."

"I'm not interested in starting anything, Master." She bowed her head, showing her submissive side.

Side? You've not got a side. This is who you are.

The wolf inside her growled at the words she thought. Her wolf didn't like to be insulted even though Dawn had a tendency to do so.

"Good. I believe you, Dawn. Now, do you believe me when I say you can trust me? I'll never hurt you, and I'll take care of you during your time with me."

What should she say?

The truth?

Lies?

Half-truths?

She settled on the truth. Lies rarely got her what she wanted. "I trust that you won't hurt me, but I don't believe we're mates. I-I-I can't trust myself to make that decision right now."

"I'm not asking you to make any decision, Dawn. Well spend some time together, and in time you'll see that I'm telling the truth."

She bit her lip and nodded. "Yes, I trust you."

Out of all of the men she knew, Daniel was always in control. He never lost his temper or used his anger against his pack. She wasn't stupid, and she'd heard his pack talk about him. None of them said anything bad. If anything, they talked about how amazing he was as an alpha, one of the best they'd ever known.

"I want you to get on the bed on your stomach and spread your arms and legs out." She hesitated for a second and then decided to do as he said. Daniel didn't push her boundaries, and he hadn't seen her naked in the year he'd been her Master.

You've not given him a chance to be a true Master to you. You fight him at every turn.

Her wolf raised her head in agreement.

She was the one in control of her body, not her wolf.

Climbing onto the bed she did as he instructed. Seconds later she felt the silk bonds wrap around her wrists followed by her ankles. Daniel took his time to secure her wrists. Her legs were spread as much as the skirt allowed. She licked her lips, wishing she could give him that other part of herself.

"You're utterly beautiful, Dawn."

He touched her ankle and withdrew his hand when his touch became too much for her. She didn't know how he knew when to release her.

"Thank you, Sir," she said.

"I didn't give you permission to speak." He slapped her ass causing her to yelp. She'd learned to make the right noises even if she didn't feel any pain. "You'll only speak when spoken to."

She kept her lips shut. Her pussy was burning, the lips of her sex drenched from the shock of his spank. His palm was large, covering as much of her ass as he could. What would it be like to give in and let him touch her? The very thought shook her a little. She'd never been curious about a more intimate touch in her life.

The tips of his fingers skimmed up her calf,

leaving her again as he moved around the room. She'd never been on a bed in his company before.

It's okay. He won't take it too far.

"You're scared of intimacy, Dawn. I want to know why, but tonight you're going to remain quiet while I talk. Do I need to use anything to keep you quiet?" he asked.

She shook her head in response.

"Good. I trust you to follow my instructions, as otherwise you'll be in trouble."

Dawn listened as he moved away from the bed, giving her more space. She turned her head, and out of the corner of her eye she watched him enter a closet. He turned on a light, but she couldn't make anything out. Was that where he kept his toys?

"You like to test me, Dawn. Your very presence teases me, and I know you enjoy it." He hummed, taking toys out of his closet. She heard the light turn off and the door close. "While you're with me, I'm going to strip down all of those walls you've kept between us. We're mates. I know you don't believe me, but we are. My wolf wants to mate you, claim you. I'm keeping him at bay until we've sorted through this problem. For your stay we're going to set down some ground rules." He placed something on the bed. The bonds stopped her from moving to look.

Gritting her teeth, she scrunched her eyes closed to stop herself from asking him what it was.

"Some of my rules you're not going to like, but you're going to do it because I will follow through with my threat, Dawn. Right, you can speak when I ask you a question, understood?"

"Yes, Master."

"Good. Now, you may count as well."

Whack!

His palm landed on her ass.

"One," she said, loving the feel of his hand on her ass even if she couldn't feel the bite of pain his touch should have created.

Whack!

"Two."

She expected his hand to land on her rump again. It never did. He'd stopped touching her. Opening her eyes, she gasped to see him staring at her.

"Am I hurting you?"

"No."

"You like pain?"

Dawn opened her mouth to dispute him then stopped. *Don't lie to him. He always knows when I lie.*

"Yes." Was it really a lie? He could probably maim her and she wouldn't feel it.

"How much pain?"

She licked her lips, wondering what to say to him. There was a point inside her when she started to hate what was happening, and it left her feeling sick. The men she was with never gave her what she needed, and she never found what she was looking for.

"Dawn!"

He spoke her name in a warning.

"I like a lot of pain." She let out a breath as the semblance of a truth spilled from her lips. After all, she went hunting for pain but never found it.

"Are you speaking the truth?" he asked.

"Yes."

"Do you know how much pain you like?"

She shook her head.

"I asked you a direct question."

"Some of the pain has drawn blood." She felt her cheeks heating. Would he be able to see her embarrassment?

"I can smell your embarrassment, pet. Why are you embarrassed?"

"It's wrong to draw blood. Something's wrong with me. None of the people in my father's pack need what I need. I'm not normal." *None of them are searching for pain in the hope of finally feeling it.* No one knew what she'd done by killing that man. Did she do the right thing in taking his life? She didn't know. He had hurt other people, but did he deserve to die at her hand, or claw?

There were no easy answers for her. What would Daniel think of her when he found out the truth? Would he be repulsed and wish he'd never given her a chance? She was a defective mate.

He pushed some of her hair out of the way, leaning in close. "Did I ever say I was looking for someone normal? You're perfect the way you are."

Daniel moved away from her. "You're going to be getting naked when you're with me, and I don't expect to hear any complaints from you. We'll both be naked, and we're going to explore this between us."

She didn't want him to see her naked.

Dawn cried out as he slapped her ass with a cane. If only she could feel the pain.

"Three." She screamed the word. He struck hard with the cane, or at least, she imagined it was hard. No pain blossomed on her bottom, but her clit swelled because of his presence. Daniel never failed to arouse her.

Chapter Three

Daniel struck her twice more with the cane surprised that she kept up with the counting. She was such a good sub. He wouldn't trade her in for anyone.

She likes pain to the point of bleeding.

In some transitions from human to wolf, the line between pleasure and pain got switched. He heard of some men and women who could take so much pain they could be on the verge of death and it wouldn't affect them emotionally. The workings of a wolf body surprised him. Dawn wasn't strange or different from many of them. She was afraid, untutored, and alone. Her wolf was torn in two between wanting him and being afraid. He wasn't an idiot. Dawn had done something to cause this problem.

Putting the cane down on the floor, he stared at her body hating the sight of the clothes. He'd give anything to have her spread out and naked, her dark flesh revealed for him to touch, caress, or punish.

Wait, have patience. She'll be ours.

His wolf passed along the walls of his mind. They wanted to claim the female in front of him. He picked up the paddle. This one had holes inside, and he brought it down on her ass. He made sure to strike hard enough for pain but not enough to bruise.

It was almost impossible to use a paddle without bruising, but he didn't give her everything.

She cried out, screaming the numbers he wanted to hear. The scent of her arousal filled the room, and his wolf howled inside his mind. They wanted to slide between her thighs and lick her creamy cunt. She'd be dripping wet the time he got his mouth around her clit, swallowing down her juice. The smell of her pussy alone was driving him crazy. His cock thickened, imagining what it would feel like to her wrapped around his length.

Don't push.

Once he was done with the paddle, he decided not to use the whip. Sitting on the edge of the bed, he touched her back. The shirt she wore was soaked in sweat.

"When you see me enter a room, I want you to present to me. This will be the case inside my house. If we ever have company, you do not need to present to me. The only exception to this rule is when we're outside. Do you understand?"

"Yes, I understand," she said.

Daniel pushed some of her hair that had fallen over her face out of the way. Her beautiful brown eyes stared back at him. She didn't smile, but then, Dawn rarely smiled. Before their time was over, he wanted to get that smile on her face.

"We're going to talk about your past and your future. My house is open and surrounded by land for us to run freely. If you think to run from me then I'll tell your father the truth."

"This is blackmail," she said.

He slapped her ass. "I hadn't finished speaking." Daniel glared at her before continuing with what he was talking about. "As I was saying, if you run from me then I'll tell your father. You do anything to ruin this and I'll make sure to ruin you as well. It's blackmail, but try living for a year with knowing your mate is being a stubborn woman."

Her gaze left him, and he gripped her chin to force her to look at him.

"I'm sorry," she said.

"Good." Daniel got to his feet and removed the silk tying her to the bed. He'd love to keep her bound, but it wasn't what he had to do.

Once she was released and sitting up, he noticed she didn't rub at her wrists or ankles like other women did. "Call your father."

He pointed to the phone at the side of the bed.

"If I use that phone he'll know where the call is coming from. I may as well tell him where I am."

"It's a personal and private line, Dawn. Untraceable. He can try to find you, but unless you give a location, he won't." He folded his arms over his chest and watched her type in her father's number.

"Hey, Dad, it's me, Dawn."

"What's the matter, honey? Do you need a ride or something?" her father asked. Daniel was able to listen to the conversation. Wolves had brilliant hearing.

"No, no. I just wanted to let you know I wouldn't be back home for a couple of days. I'm going to stay with a couple of girlfriends and have some fun." She looked up at him.

Daniel waited.

"Honey, are you sure you're okay? You don't sound fine."

"I'm sure. I'm fine. Nothing is wrong with me. I'm calling so you don't worry and send out a search party." She forced a laugh. Daniel watched her knowing in his heart he needed to fix what had gone wrong during her transition.

"Okay, honey. I'll see you when you get back. Keep in touch."

"I will."

They said their goodbyes, and she put the phone back in the cradle.

"Do you feel pain?" he asked. He didn't know why, but his gut was telling him something wasn't right. Every other sub would be wincing at the spanking he'd given her, yet Dawn didn't respond or show any sign of being aware of it.

She looked up at him. "Yes, I feel pain. My dad doesn't have a true mate of his own. He settled down for the strongest female in the pack. She's my mother."

"You've never mentioned your mother."

"She's not the kind of person I like to talk about." She dropped her gaze again, and he sensed the hate inside her.

"Why?"

She blew out a breath before running her fingers through her hair. "I don't know. I just don't."

"You don't mention her, and you didn't ask about her. Why?"

"My mom, she's not the greatest example of a mother."

Daniel waited for her to continue. "You're not going to say anymore?" he asked when she showed no signs of saying anything more.

"No. My mom is not a topic we need to discuss."

The fact she didn't want to discuss her mother meant it was a more important topic to talk about. Daniel stayed silent, filing the information away 'til later.

"Okay, right, grab your bag. We're going to head to my place," he said.

"Now?"

"Yes." He took her hand in his, and he walked toward the bar. She didn't fight him as he placed her on the stool. "Stay here. I'll be back to collect you shortly."

Leaving her alone, he went into the far security office where he found Jake staring at the screens.

"I need you to spread the word that until further notice my house is off limits to the pack. Tell them if they need me they're to call me and I'll deal with whatever problems they have."

"Why can't we come to the house?" Jake asked.

"I'm taking Dawn with me."

"You've finally got her to admit you're mates?"

Daniel shook his head. "Will you do this for me?"

"Consider it done. I'll put the word out immediately." Jake took out his cell phone and started to type. "Are you sure about this?"

He stopped to look at his friend. "She's my other half, Jake. I'm sure, and I'm going to fix whatever has been broken inside her." He looked at the security cameras. "Please keep this place in order." He nodded at the men then left the room.

Walking back to the bar he watched Dawn sipping from a straw. She always ordered a soda, a clear cream soda. Her eyes were closed as she enjoyed the taste of her drink.

Running a hand down his face, he wondered if he was doing the right thing in taking her back home with him.

Ours.

Dawn was his mate, the other half of him, and he'd be damned if he let her get away. He touched her shoulder as he approached. She jerked at his touch yet didn't pull away.

"Finish your drink and then we're going."

"Can I ask you a question?" Her brown eyes were wide as she stared at him.

"Yes," he said, taking a seat.

"Why now? Why wait a year to put me in this position?"

He smiled. "I've finally had enough of our games. You're holding back from me, and that I don't like. I've played it your way and gotten fuck all out of it. It's time to play it my way, and I'm going to do that now."

She finished her drink leaving a tiny amount of soda in the bottom.

"Why haven't you finished your drink?" he asked.

"I have."

Daniel pointed at the remnants she left in the glass. "If I drink that it'll make a noise with the straw, and if I pull out the straw, it'll make a mess on the side."

He stood taking her hand. There was more to that explanation. His gut was telling him he wouldn't like what she had to say.

****

Daniel's house was old and huge. He stopped outside a large iron gate and typed in a code that opened those imposing gates. She looked behind her to see the gates close up after him. They shut closed, trapping her inside the grounds with Daniel. There were worse people to be locked up with.

Mother's one of them.

She shut off her thoughts and turned to face the front. He drove down a really long driveway that was surrounded by large, thick trees.

"The house has been in the family for generations."

"Were you all wolves?" she asked, glancing toward him.

"Yes. Some of my ancestors married humans and moved away and others stayed close."

"Where are your parents now?" she asked.

"They're enjoying a much needed vacation. They're exploring Europe, visiting with some packs they've not had the pleasure of seeing in years." He tapped the steering wheel as he talked.

"How did you take over as alpha?"

He smiled. "My dad told me it was time to take

the spot. He was getting old, and he said a true alpha knows when to step aside and bring in a new one. I was the next in line, and so I stepped up to the role."

"What about the other men in your pack? Weren't they annoyed to be passed over by you?"

"Some of the men challenged me in battle. I won, but I always refused to do battle to the death. I don't want anyone's blood on my hands."

She tensed at his words.

I've got blood on my hands.

Staring out of the window she gasped as his house came into sight. It was so huge she doubted she'd have to see him for days at a time. They could play hide and seek and still miss each other.

"This is your house?" she asked, amazed.

"Yeah. The pack can come and go as they please. Don't worry, they know not to come here until further notice."

She climbed out of the car once he brought it to a stop.

"You're amazed? Did you think I lived somewhere small?" he asked, coming to stand beside her.

"I was thinking a cabin somewhere out in the sticks. I didn't even imagine this."

"Does it make my mating claim more appealing?" he asked.

She turned to look at him. "I'm not a gold digger, and neither do I hope to make a claim on anything."

"I didn't say you did. Sometimes, female wolves like to see that they can be taken care of. Does your wolf like what she sees?" He stood right behind her with his palm lightly resting on her back.

Dawn paused as she listened to her wolf.

"No, we don't think you're a better catch or anything. We're worried what you owning this big house means."

"Why would it mean anything?"

"You'd be surprised how dangerous large houses and big men are." She stared up at the house feeling … happy, safe? Dawn didn't know which emotion to trust or to savor. Daniel wouldn't hurt her. He'd been her Dom for a year and he never left her scared, nervous but never scared.

"I'm going to know all of those secrets you're hiding," he said.

"They're not secrets." *They're just memories of a time I'd like to forget.*

He leaned in close. She felt his breath across her cheek. Her body tightened with the heat of him. Inside her wolf started to growl, wanting to get a little closer to his body. What would it be like to strip naked and turn? To run with him in the wild of the forest without anyone to hear her thoughts? She'd stopped running in the forests back at home as the connection of the pack allowed them to access her thoughts if she was close enough. They would all be repulsed by her if they knew the truth. She didn't hold any doubt that they'd cast her out as if she didn't exist in her parents' world.

"There are always secrets in this world, pet." He dropped a kiss to her cheek, and for the first time she was charmed by his touch. No one ever took the time to touch her, hold her, reassure her.

All thoughts of her mother were cut off.

"I don't have any changes of clothes," she said, turning to look at him.

"You don't need any clothes. We're alone, and that's the way it's going to stay." He took her hand leading her up the multiple steps to get to the main door. She watched him pull out a set of keys and start to unlock the large door.

"Don't you have any other alphas trying to take over your territory?" she asked.

"No. I treat all packs with the respect they deserve, and I demand they treat me as such."

Her father didn't allow any other pack to walk through his territory. If another wolf from another pack walked on his land, he'd give the wolf a beating. She had grown tired of watching men and women beg. For a woman, her mother delivered the beating as her father didn't believe in hurting a woman. Her mother never had a problem with causing pain.

"They come to me for permission to enter my lands, and I grant it to them. I don't cause fights that are unnecessary. My pack likes to live in the open without fear of being approached by others. I make sure they're all taken care of." Daniel switched on a light as she entered his home.

The door closed, and the sound echoed throughout the old house as if it was a sign of approaching doom.

We're trapped!

There was no getting out of this house until Daniel was satisfied. Would it be so hard to agree to his claim of being her mate? She truly didn't know what to think about his claim. Dawn was torn in two between wanting his claim more than her next breath and then scared of accepting his claim.

Once he knew the truth, would he really want her? No man truly wanted a murderer for a mate.

She cut the thoughts off, staring at Daniel as he turned back to her. He slid the bolts into place locking them inside the dominating house.

"For tonight, we're not going to do anything. We're going to enjoy some good food and drink, and then we'll go to bed."

"Where will I sleep?" she asked.

"Where I tell you to." He walked down the long entrance hall, taking a left. She hurried her steps to keep up with him. Considering the age of the house, the scents were sweet, charming.

Whoever lived here they were happy. The house smelled of happiness, of peace. It was such a strange scent to have around the house. She rushed toward him, following him through three more rooms before they made it to the kitchen.

"The house has multiple rooms for the pack. They do visit, and when they do I like for them to make themselves at home. Unfortunately with wolves, they fight. I've got four television rooms so there's no fight over the remote or what they watch." She chuckled, imagining an argument turning heated in the sight of a remote. Ravaging wolves, attacking each other just because they didn't want to watch a television program. "You can laugh all you want. It's happened."

He entered a large kitchen. She stopped to admire the room, which was set in an old country style fit with a porcelain sink. The island in the center was large, yet it would fit many people sitting around helping.

"Again, the kitchen is large enough for the whole pack."

"How do you keep this place cleaned?" she asked.

"I've got a wolf who's a little obsessive when it comes to cleaning. She makes sure everything is clean when she comes to visit. Also, I make the pack clean up after themselves. I won't have shit lying around because they're too fucking lazy to do their shit." He moved toward the fully stocked fridge. She smelled the freshness in the vegetables and the meat inside. Had he planned for her to be spending time with him?

No, he's got a pack who also needs to eat.

"Do you cook?" she asked.

"Yeah, I cook, and I occasionally clean. I also do the washing." He turned to offer her a smile.

"Are we in a scene right now?" she asked, unsure about the proper protocol she needed to give him.

"Would you feel safer being in a scene?" he asked.

She shook her head. "No."

"Then we're not in a scene. We're just two people, Daniel and Dawn for tonight."

Relief swamped her. She could handle simply being a woman sharing a meal with Daniel.

Mate.

He bent over to grab something out of the fridge, and she checked out his ass. It was tight and firm.

"You're checking out my ass," he said, smiling as he turned to face her.

"Am not."

"Don't worry, Dawn, I won't put you over my knee."

She saw he was teasing her and couldn't help but smile. "I like the thought of going over your knee."

He laughed, throwing his head back.

Yes, she could handle being alone with him for a few days.

Chapter Four

Daniel started to cut the chicken, and with each inhale he smelled Dawn sitting at the island. She smelled like sweet citrus, addictive and something he wanted to smell over and over again. He washed his hands before walking toward the pantry. Daniel grabbed the spices and noodles he needed to finish off dinner.

"Do you want a drink?" he asked, spreading his ingredients out over the side.

"Sure."

He passed her over a soda from the fridge. She took the can from his hands. Their fingers touched, and he didn't want to let her go. Drawing his attention away from her, he started to cook.

"Would you like some help? I love to cook," she said, standing beside him.

"You love to cook?"

"Yes, and bake but my hips protest a little to that." She rested a hand on her hip.

Staring down the length of her body, Daniel couldn't find a single reason to complain about the woman in front of him. She was sex on legs, and he wouldn't change her for the world.

"You're perfect, and don't let anyone else tell you otherwise." He reached out to touch her cheek. Cupping her jaw, he ran a thumb over her plump lips. "You're beautiful, and I don't give a fuck what others think. You're perfect." He leaned in close, brushing his lips against hers.

She gasped but didn't move away. He looked into her wide gaze as he teased her lips with his tongue.

Neither of them said a word as he slowly slid inside her mouth, meeting her tongue with his. Wrapping his other hand around her waist, he pulled her close to his body, moaning at the feel of her curves next to his. She was perfection in his arms. He never wanted to let her go.

She met his tongue with her own. The danced together, deepening the kiss, Daniel smelled the mating heat coming out of him. He wanted inside her with her pussy blooming beneath him.

He withdrew from her before the mating need took over and he wouldn't be able to control his actions.

"Why did you stop?" she asked. Her hands were on his shoulders, gripping him.

"If we don't stop I won't be able to stop what happens next. I need to claim you, Dawn. You're my mate even if you don't like the truth or believe it. There's only so much I can take before I do something I'll regret."

She released his shoulders. "I'm sorry."

"Don't be sorry. I want to prove to you that we're mated. I'm not going to do anything to destroy that trust." His cock protested against the front of his jeans. Fuck, he craved her. All he wanted to do was bend her over the kitchen island and fuck her raw. She was aroused by him, which gave him some pleasure. "Start marinating the meat."

Dawn grabbed the strips of chicken and added them to a bowl while he started to add the spices to the mix. They laughed as he got most of the spices on her hands rather than the meat. He listened to her laugh, loving the change within her. In Kinkster's she was always a little withdrawn. Inside his home, she was starting to open up and flourish. If he gave her enough time would she agree to his claiming? There was only so much his wolf could take.

"Right, Chef, I'm rubbing the chicken. What do you need to do?" she asked.

Her eyes glinted with humor. Charmed, he

pressed a kiss to her nose then turned back to the stove. He put a pot onto boil adding noodles for their chicken. They started to boil, and he gave them a stir.

Dawn washed her hands, coming to stand beside him while he heated oil. Together, they worked as a team to make food. She added food while he tossed it around with a spoon.

Neither of them spoke, but his gaze caught the sight of her hard, erect nipples. Again, his cock started to pound at the sight. The vision of her naked on his bed wouldn't leave his mind.

Trust, this is about building trust.

For the next ten minutes they cooked dinner, and the scents of the spicy chicken filled the air. His stomach rumbled with the need to feed.

Sitting next to each other they ate in comfortable silence.

"This is amazing," she said, twirling some noodles onto her fork. "You know how to cook."

"You wouldn't have thought that from my first attempt at spicy chicken noodles. I vomited for three days afterwards."

She chuckled, covering her mouth as she did. "You're joking. I don't believe you."

"I didn't cook the chicken properly. I tell you, it was the worst couple of days for me."

"Okay, I can believe that." They cleaned away their mess, and he put the spices away. When they were done, he led her out of the kitchen and moved toward the stairs.

"I'll give you the grand tour tomorrow. For now I think it'll be good if you get a good night's sleep." He took hold of her hand, gritting his teeth as his wolf started to pace within his mind. His wolf knew what he wanted, and that was Dawn.

She followed him upstairs, and he decided to stay on the first floor rather than go up to the main bedroom on the fifth floor. The attic space was large, and he kept a lot of his ancestors' belongings up there. He opened the door at the end of the long corridor that was next to his.

"This is where you'll be staying." He turned the light on revealing the large four poster bed with white lace hanging from each post. "Here is the wardrobe." He opened the walk-in space, showing the light switch to turn it on. There were a couple of sets of shirts and jeans. He had a tendency to buy clothes for his pack when needed. Daniel showed her the bathroom then opened the double doors onto the small veranda overlooking the garden. "In the morning you can watch the sunrise, and it's a truly beautiful sight." He closed the doors, locking them and pulling the drapes over the windows. "This is where I'll be sleeping." He opened the connecting door and turned the lights on.

"How come you don't have any of those clapping light things? My dad installed them in our house," Dawn said. "It makes it much easier as you just clap your hands." She showed him by clapping her hands.

"I did get them installed, but my pack are, erm, very active with sex. The lights kept turning on with their smacking bodies as they fucked. They asked for me to switch back to this." He flicked the switch letting the lights go off then on.

She laughed. "I can see why you changed."

"If you need me in the night don't hesitate to come to me. I'll be happy to see you." He closed the distance between them. Dawn tilted her head back, and he gazed down into the beauty of her brown eyes. "Tomorrow we'll talk about you and discover what your pain level is."

"I don't think that's a good idea."

"We'll start with a run. The moon is a couple of weeks away, but going for a run can be just as fun." He dropped a kiss to her lips. "Good night, Dawn."

She took a step back, closing the door behind her.

Our mate is in the next room. Claim her, fuck her, take her.

He ignored the wolf inside him, taking a deep breath to calm his body. He wasn't going to be going anywhere to put his woman in danger.

Leaving the scent of her lurking behind the door, he walked into his bathroom, closing the door. He grabbed a match and took it to the lavender candle he kept on hand for whenever he needed to bring focus to his thoughts and senses. The lavender helped to calm the wolf within him.

The beast inside him calmed, finally listening to reason as he took deep breaths.

She needs to trust us.

He didn't want a mate who was with him out of an obligation. The mate he wanted for himself was not going to be there because she had to. He wanted Dawn to fall in love with him, to be with him because they were a devoted mated couple.

The fact she liked to be dominated eased his thoughts. One of his biggest fears was to find a woman who didn't share his need for kink. She was not only submissive, but she liked pain. What Dawn didn't know was he liked to give pain so long as it wasn't the kind that emotionally or mentally affected the woman he was with.

Take a breath, and delve into it tomorrow.

****

Sliding under the covers, Dawn stared up at the ceiling. She frowned as she saw the mirror above her. Kinky. Underneath the silk covers she wasn't wearing a stitch of clothing. Gripping the edge of the blanket, she stared at herself wondering what the hell she was doing. When she was at home with the rest of the pack her room was half the size of the one she was staying in. She hadn't moved out of her house as the pack wouldn't accept that of her until she found her mate. Her father didn't trust her out on her own, and so she remained with him and her mother.

She shuddered thinking about her mother.

Don't think about her.

Pushing her mother aside, she focused instead on the man in the bedroom next to hers. He wasn't going to let her hide from him. The pack was easier to hide from back at home. Her father was the only one in the whole pack who demanded her presence at dinner or during a run. She rarely changed into a wolf even though he asked for her to be there. Her father loved her; her mother despised her. And Daniel? She didn't know what Daniel felt about her. There were times throughout the year where she thought he was going to cross the line and take what he wanted. He never did, and her trust in him began to build.

He's our mate.

Was it worth arguing with him anymore? She couldn't trust herself to be around him. Her search for pain had put her in scary situations. Other men she'd been with had considered her a freak. There was no way she could bear for Daniel to know the truth. She was defective. It sucked that she wanted Daniel and yet was scared because of what she had done in her past. What would he think when he knew the truth?

Staring at her reflection she once again pushed all of the negative thoughts aside, wishing for some kind of change within her. Finding a mate should have awakened something inside, yet all she felt was a consuming dread.

With a mate, she'd have to finally come clean about who she was. Daniel was a Master, but he wasn't the kind of Master she needed. He spanked. He was tame compared to what she needed. Part of her wondered if the reason she couldn't feel pain was because the men she'd been with wouldn't hurt her hard enough. The image of the man who'd left her bleeding entered her mind. No, it couldn't be that. She should have felt something.

You're sick.

She pushed the blanket off her body and stared at her nakedness. Would he be repulsed by the way she looked? Food had always been part of her comfort when her emotions got so bad. She loved eating, cooking and eating. Her legs were thick with a small hint of cellulite, but she rarely wore anything but skirts and never revealed her skin to anyone. She kept her pussy bare, and the brown lips of her sex glistened with arousal. Daniel's scent was everywhere in the room driving her crazy with need.

With thick hips, large breasts, and the occasional glimmer of a stretch mark, in the mirror her body didn't look that bad. She was lying down, so maybe gravity was taking over to make her look good. Her brown hair was spread out on the white pillow.

Mates.

She didn't know if she could be this open with Daniel. He wouldn't let her hide.

The house is large enough. We can hide.

Pressing a hand to her face, she tried to calm down her rioting thoughts, wishing something would happen to save her.

The memory of his hand spanking her ass filled her mind. Opening her eyes, she spread her legs and tilted her hips to see the lips of her pussy open up. She went to her knees and dropped the drapes to create a little more privacy for herself. Settling on the bed, she watched as she caressed her hand down her body. She touched her nipples, tugging on the hard brown buds until they were erect and pushing up.

She glided her hand down her stomach, feeling the muscles in her stomach tighten at the contact.

Dawn pressed a finger to her clit, touching the swollen bud as she pinched her nipples. She squeezed her nipple between her nails hoping to feel at least some pain and getting none. Gasping, she moved her hips with her hand.

What would Daniel do if he saw her now? She didn't know what he'd do, and that excited her as much as anything else.

Leaving her clit she pushed two fingers inside her, opening her fingers to make it a little tighter. She sucked her lips in to contain the moan threatening to get out.

"Do you think I can't smell you," Daniel said.

She gasped, withdrawing her hand and loosening the hold on her nipple. Going to her knees, she shuffled to the edge of the bed and opened the lace. Daniel stood in the doorway between their rooms.

"I can smell and hear what you're doing. I didn't give you permission to play with yourself."

He stood completely naked. His cock was rock hard and stood out in front of him. The size of him made her mouth go dry. There was no way he'd fit inside a woman and it be comfortable.

"I'm sorry."

"No, you're not. If you wanted to touch yourself then you should have come to me for permission to do so."

"I didn't know we were in a scene."

Daniel sighed. "We're not in a scene, Dawn. You

need some strict rules in your life. You keep everything at arms'-length, hiding behind your walls of frost and depression." He folded his arms, staring at her. "This can't wait until morning. We're going to have this discussion now." He stood facing her, making no move to put some clothes on.

"Can you please get dressed?" It would give her time to grab a robe and not be completely naked in front of him.

"So you can hide from me? I don't think so." He stayed where he was. "We're going to see each other naked. I don't see why it shouldn't be now."

"That's easy for you to say. You're like a god while I'm blubber."

He glared at her. "Step off the bed now!"

His voice deepened. Dawn stared at him wondering if she could simply go back to bed and sleep without him ordering her around.

"Don't disobey me, Dawn. I was willing to wait until tomorrow, and all you've done is test me. I don't like being tested." He stayed still even as his voice travelled throughout the room. The Alpha inside him raised the hairs all over her body. Her clit swelled at the command within his voice. Slowly, keeping the lace in front of her, she stepped off the bed.

"Drop the lace. You're not hiding from me." He walked toward the door and flicked the light, illuminating the whole room. There was no hiding anymore. He made sure of that.

"This is unfair."

"Unfair is having a mate for a whole year denying you. Unfair is that mate fingering herself instead of coming to her Dom. Don't even begin to tell me what's unfair or not. You'll not like what I've got to say." He folded his arms once again.

His gaze was on hers, waiting.

"I can't do this."

"Yes, you can. If you don't I promise you there'll be a severe punishment, one you won't like."

What wouldn't she like? She'd pushed Daniel the entire year they'd known each other. He had every right to be mad and punish her. How far would he go to consider her punished?

The uncertainty was too much for her. She gripped the lace tightly, before slowly stepping from behind the security of the lace.

She kept her head bowed and pressed her palms together in an attempt to control her shaking. Letting a man see her naked took a lot of effort for her. She was used to pushing her skirt up and having the man suck her nipples through the shirt. Her entire sexual life was appalling. The only man who'd seen her naked were dead. She'd let him hurt her in the worst kind of ways.

"Look at me, Dawn."

Glancing up at him, she didn't know what she expected to find. Would he lose his erection? Show any signs that he hated what he saw?

Again she was in a strange territory for her.

His cock remained rock hard. He'd not deflated or grown flaccid since seeing her naked.

"What did you expect to see?" he asked. He didn't make a move to touch his cock.

"What do you mean?"

"Don't play dumb. I'm not stupid. I see in your eyes that you were expecting something from me. What?"

The desire to lie struck her again.

Don't lie to him. He'll know.

"I didn't expect you to be hard."

"Why wouldn't I be hard?"

She stared at the tip of his cock. He was glistening, aroused.

"Look at me," she said, releasing her hands so not an inch of her was covered. "I'm not beautiful. I eat too much, and you're perfect. You should be a model or something."

His arms remained folded over his chest. Neither of them said a word. He kept looking at her. There was something in his gaze that she couldn't quite put her finger on. "Get on your knees," he said. The words were spoken slowly, with menace, leaving no mistake of his anger.

Shit, what had she done?

Chapter Five

Daniel was pissed off with her lack of self-esteem. Didn't she know how beautiful she was?

"What?" she asked.

"Get on your knees. Don't make me repeat myself. We're going to deal with this the only way you know how." He watched her struggle with his demand. There was no way he intended to help her. The moment he scented her arousal he thought he was losing his mind. When he heard her moans, he'd gotten angry. She wouldn't let him touch her intimately, and yet she'd do whatever she could to satisfy herself. How many times had she left him in an aroused state while she took care of her own needs? He hadn't been with another woman since she entered his world.

"Daniel?"

"No. To you I'm not Daniel. You'll call me Sir or Master, I don't care which. I was going to do this slowly for you to trust me, but we're going to start now. You're my sub. In the mornings you will wake up at seven, go to the bathroom, and you'll be waiting for me by seven thirty beside your bed. I expect you on your knees, ready to serve me." He took a step closer. Dawn was on her knees, her head bent in the perfect pose.

There was something about a submissive woman in that pose that turned him on. His cock was aching on the point of pain. The scent of her arousal filled the air. His wolf wanted to do nothing more than stake his claim. Daniel made sure he stayed in complete control.

"You'll eat breakfast with me. We'll train together, and you're going to become my sub. For the next month I'm going to prove to you that you're my mate." He gripped her chin as she started to shake her head. Forcing her to look at him, he stared into her eyes.

"You're my mate, Dawn. In time you'll see the truth. We're going to get to the bottom of those secrets you've kept hidden."

"You don't know what you're doing."

"Baby, I've been a Dom for over ten years. I've got more experience with stubborn little subs than you do with Doms. You're nothing but a baby compared to me, and I'm going to prove it to you over and over again." She stopped fighting him. Her teeth bit down onto her lip. "Stop that." He pulled her lip from between her teeth. "You think you know what true pain is, but you've got no idea what's really wrong with you. Don't worry. I can deal with you."

He reached down, grabbing her arm and drawing her up toward his body.

She fought him, and he continued to hold her. Her arousal intensified. Not once did she scream for him to stop or tell him no.

Pressing her to the bed, he grabbed her hands pressing them above the bed, holding both of her hands in one of his. With his free hand he glided his hand down her body.

"You could have come to me and I'd know exactly what to do to bring you off."

She laughed, the sound harsh and bitter. "You'd be the first man."

He smiled. "No other man has ever brought you to orgasm. Baby, you're in for a treat. Giving women orgasms is a skill I learned early." Leaning down, he sucked her tight brown nipple into his mouth. He didn't give her time to grow accustomed to his touch, biting down on the hard bud.

Dawn cried out, arching up against his hold. Her strength was no match for his. Holding her hands down to the bed, he pressed a palm to her stomach keeping her in place as he tortured the bud nearest him.

Still, she didn't beg him to stop or ask him to go easy on her. She screamed her pleasure. Clearly, the pain brought more arousal from her. The musky scent filled the air, making his mouth water and his cock pulse with the need to be inside her. He wouldn't be fucking her tonight. No, he'd take care of his woman's needs before he even dealt with his own. Daniel wouldn't be dealing with his own arousal until he was behind closed doors.

Flicking her nipple, he glanced up her body to see her eyes squeezed shut. Withdrawing from the bud he blew on it. Her nipple tightened, and she gasped. He leaned over her body and did the exact same to the other. Once again she fought him, her lips remaining closed other than to gasp or scream. He drew the nipple tight, biting down to the point where he was close to breaking skin.

Wolves had a higher pain threshold, and they could withstand a lot more pain than most humans. Dawn was showing him something had changed within during her first transition into a wolf. Even wolves who liked pain would be protesting a little.

There was nothing coming from Dawn. He liked to give pain and punish his woman, but drawing blood was not what he hoped to do.

Daniel needed to know what happened to her during her transition.

"Please," she said, begging him.

"Don't beg me, pet. You had a chance to beg. Now, you're all mine, and you get what I give you." He changed his attention between both of her breasts, biting and sucking the hard buds into his mouth.

He straddled her waist to get closer to her. She arched up against him. Throughout it all, her arousal only increased, telling him more about her. The wolf inside her was humming in approval. She liked him and wanted the mating.

When they turned, he'd be able to hear her thoughts and know some of her secrets. He wondered what he'd have to do to get her to agree to change with him.

Moving off her body, he ran his fingers down her body to rest at her naked pussy. The lips of her sex were soaking wet from her arousal. Sliding his finger through her wet slit, he pinched her clit causing more pain.

Slowly, he moved down to press inside her cunt. The walls of her pussy gripped his digits, begging for him to stay within her. Pumping his fingers in and out of her, he sucked on her nipples.

She writhed underneath him, thrusting her pelvis up to his touch.

He took his time to torture her, drawing out the pleasure.

Dawn was so close to orgasm. He removed his hand from her pussy and licked his fingers.

"What are you doing?" she asked.

"I'm tasting my mate." He licked her cream loving the taste like he knew he would. "Just like I thought, you taste perfect."

She moaned. "Please, Sir, touch me."

"Are you close to coming?"

"Yes."

"We'll see how close you are. Keep your hands above your head. If you move them I'll punish you." He'd make sure she was bound in sleep so that she couldn't touch her pussy. There were more ways to punish a little pain sub without putting her over the knee and spanking her. Like he said, he had more experience with stubborn little subs than she ever would with Doms.

He released her hands and kept his gaze on her.

"Test me, Dawn, and you'll regret it."

"I won't, Sir."

"Good." Sliding to the floor, he cupped her tits, feeling the rounded tips fill his palms. They were so big that he couldn't hold them within his hands. He pinched both nipples together. Dawn's legs slid open revealing her creamy cunt to his gaze.

Closing the distance between them, he sucked her clit into his mouth.

She screamed, jerking on the bed. Her hands didn't touch him.

He pinched her nipples a little tighter, rubbing the nubs afterward as he sucked, bit, and flicked her clit.

Her cum was soaking his chin, and he drank it up.

"Put your legs over my shoulders," he said, waiting for her to do as he ordered. Her legs opened a little wider.

Pressing his tongue into her cunt, he glided his tongue up to circle her clit. He used his nails to pinch her nipples at the same time he bit her clit. The pain along with the pleasure must have set her off as she screamed out her release, filling his mouth with her cum.

He moaned, drinking her down, loving the taste. She rubbed her pussy all over his face.

When he was finished, he climbed up the bed smiling down at her. Daniel didn't wipe the juices from his chin.

"Get in bed and remember my rules tomorrow."

"What about you?" she asked.

He slapped her ass as she started to shuffle into bed. "I'll deal with myself. Stubborn little subs don't get to touch my cock." He walked toward the open connecting door. Before closing it, he turned back to look at Dawn. "Remember, Dawn, I was the first man to bring you to orgasm. I can do that every night without effort.

Your pussy is so fucking tasty."

Closing the door behind him, he walked toward the bathroom. Staring at his reflection he saw the color change of his eyes. His wolf was close to the surface. Climbing into the shower, he turned the freezing cold water on waiting for the temperature to take care of his problem.

The water cascaded over his body doing little to relieve the ache her body had caused. Wrapping his fingers around his cock, he growled. The taste of her pussy had been exquisite. She'd be a delight to have by his side to love, to claim, to fuck.

Ours.

Not only was he going to claim Dawn, he intended to own her. Closing his eyes, he pictured her creamy brown cunt, begging for his cock. She'd look so fucking good taking his dick into her body.

He was big compared to her. Daniel would need to take his time to get her ready to take his cock. She needed to be wet enough, slick, and he'd need to go slow.

She likes pain.

Maybe he wouldn't need to go too slow. He could work with Dawn. First, he needed to strip down those walls she'd built up around her heart and her emotions. To a lot of people, Dawn was cut off, emotionless, depressed. He knew it wasn't the case. There was no way a woman with that much passion locked up inside could be filled with nothing. He was going to bring her out, learn every part of her, and then show her how she could be herself around him. There was no shame in submitting to her mate or to embrace a life of a submissive.

Working from the root down to the tip, Daniel fucked his fist, moaning as the pleasure built inside him.

His seed spurted out coating the floor of the cold

shower. He watched it wash away. The orgasm was nothing like what he wanted to feel, but once he was inside Dawn, he just knew it was going to be explosive.
****

Dawn woke up to the alarm beside her bed ringing. She frowned, reaching out to press on the button to turn the blasted machine off. Staring at the time she let out a groan. It was seven o'clock. Who in their right mind would set the alarm for seven? The unfairness of it wasn't even funny.

Suddenly, the memory of last night rushed over her. Sitting up in bed, she glanced around the room. The lace curtains were shut apart from the ones at the base of the bed showing the door connecting her room to Daniel's. Her heart raced as her pussy flooded with warmth from what he had done to her last night. Glancing down at her nipples she saw they were slightly bruised. Her skin was dark, yet she saw the off purple of the bruise. Licking her lips, she climbed out of the bed and padded toward the doors. Sliding the curtain open she gasped at the view of the garden. There was a waterfall display at the forefront, which opened up into the most beautiful forest.

He warned us to be ready by seven thirty.

She checked the time and released a squeal. Ten minutes had already gone. Dawn ran for the bathroom quickly doing her business on the toilet before flushing the toilet then washing her hands. Once she finished washing her hands, she found a toothbrush, brushing her teeth. She ran her fingers through her hair, hoping to put some order to the strands. Nothing was working.

With quick movements, she ran into the bedroom taking her place by the bed as the door opened connecting their bedrooms. Next time she'd set the alarm earlier so she had more time in the bathroom. She was naked, exposed, and hadn't the time to make sure she looked more appealing in the mirror. At least there wouldn't be any sleep in the corners of her eyes.

"I see you remembered what I demanded of you last night," Daniel said, stepping in front of her. He was wearing steel toe capped boots and a pair of jeans. She forced herself to keep looking at the floor even though she wanted to look at him. Why was he dressed when she wasn't allowed? "You've pleased me by not using any of the clothes in the wardrobe. I wanted you naked, but I realized I hadn't specified it. This pleases me."

She wished she'd thought about the wardrobe but then she liked the idea of pleasing him a little more.

"You may look at me."

Lifting her head she saw he wore a crisp white shirt. Disappointment filled her. She rather liked him without a shirt.

"Good morning, pet." He cupped her cheek, running a finger over her lips. "Seeing you like this pleases me." He released her face and moved past her to the drawer beside the bed. She stayed perfectly still as he got what he wanted. Seconds later he sat down on the bed. "I'm going to brush your hair for you."

He ran the brush through her hair, taking his time. When he got to knots, she was surprised how gentle he was in working them out. Her curiosity increased about him.

"You've got questions?" he asked.

"How did you know, Sir?"

"You're fidgeting. I've noticed over the year you fidget when you're curious, but otherwise you sit still like a good little sub. Ask your questions. I'm ready to listen." He continued to brush her hair. She loved the attention. Her mother hadn't been the kind of woman to spend the time brushing hair.

"Where did you learn to brush hair, Sir?" she asked. He'd given her permission to speak, but she remembered to use his title. Dawn wanted to please him further.

"I've dealt with a lot of subs. I've found many of them like this kind of attention, and it's a skill I learned to acquire. You're my mate, Dawn. I'll do whatever necessary to make you comfortable."

"I'm very comfortable," she said, smiling. "I love your touch."

"Has anyone ever taken the time to brush your hair?"

"No." She stared in front of her, resting her hands on top of her thighs.

"Get used to this. I look forward to giving you daily brushes."

She chuckled. "Sir, about last night?"

"What about it?"

"I want to apologize for my behavior."

"Are you sorry you got caught or sorry that you touched yourself without my permission?"

"Both." She'd heard him reaching orgasm last night in his shower. For the first time in her life she'd been ashamed when it came to a man. Daniel had taken care of her needs, giving her a release unlike any she'd ever felt, and he'd taken care of his own himself.

"What are you thinking?" He whispered the words against her ear causing her to jump. "I want you to know I'll be asking that question a lot. I expect you to answer me all the time. I want to know what you're thinking, feeling, and how you're dealing with our relationship. I expect total honesty."

She licked her dry lips. Honesty?

Out of all he requested, total honesty scared her more than anything.

"Dawn?"

"I was thinking how much I hated not giving you pleasure last night. I've kept us at a distance for so long." Tears filled her eyes as she thought about the emptiness of the past year. The only time she felt anything was when she was around Daniel. When she'd first heard about Kinkster's, she'd intended to go every now and then. Once she met Daniel, discovered he was her Dom, she made sure to frequent the club weekly. Her weekly visits increased to several times a week. She'd been able to hold herself back to four days a week rather than the whole seven. "I heard you in the shower. I wanted to come and pleasure you like you had me."

He paused in brushing her hair.

"I'm sorry, and I'm sorry about this last year, Sir."

Daniel brushed a kiss to her cheek. "I was thinking of you." He finished brushing her hair and stood. "It's time for breakfast. Come on, baby." He held his hand out for her to take.

Getting to her feet she followed him. She wanted to cover her body from the potential prying eyes, yet as she made her way into the kitchen, she noticed no one was around. They were alone. She was safe from anyone else looking at her. Daniel had promised her no one else would be home, and this just gave her another reason to trust him.

He took a small towel and placed it on one of the chairs. "Take a seat."

She sat on the chair. Her cheeks heated, and she wondered if he saw the embarrassment. If he did, he didn't say anything. Resting her palms on her knees she looked toward him. He was gathering stuff out of the fridge. The coffee pot was already working, filling the room with the delicious aroma.

"How do you know we're mates?" she asked, blurting the words out. Pressing a hand to her mouth, she apologized.

Daniel smiled at her. "Your scent, and my wolf is driving me crazy telling me to claim you. He knows what he wants today, tomorrow, the future. He's got it all mapped out." He chuckled.

She watched him slice into a peach and start to segment the fruit. He was making toast as well. The fresh smells made her stomach grumble. At home, she got her own breakfast, which usually consisted of cereal. Her mother wouldn't be caught dead in a kitchen. She wondered if her father knew all of their meals were prepared by a lower pack female? Dawn doubted it. Her mother wouldn't let anyone get the chance to spill the truth. She probably threatened a beating.

Minutes passed as he finished breakfast. "Doesn't your wolf recognize me?" he asked, taking a seat at the head of the table. She was beside him but away from the table. If she was to lean her arms on the table she'd look out of place.

"Yes and no. It's complicated." She tucked some hair behind her ear. The chair he sat on scraped back as he stood to his feet. The sudden movement had her tensing. He grabbed some kind of band and stood behind her. Daniel worked her hair into a ponytail. "I love your hair, but I don't want it to get in my way. I love watching your face." He took a seat again, confusing her.

He offered her a slice of peach. Staring at the fruit then at him, she frowned.

"You'll feed from my hands," he said.

Leaning forward she sucked the fruit from his fingers trying not to touch his skin. Daniel laughed. "I wash my hands. You're not going to get any diseases." For several minutes he fed her different slices of fruit, sipping his coffee and reading the paper. The only attention he paid her was with the fruit he offered up.

Was she invisible?

Gripping the edge of her seat, she took more fruit. When the bowl was empty he buttered some toast and tore the bread apart. Again, she had to take the food from his fingers. Slowly, the anger started to ebb away to be replaced with comfort. She liked taking food from his offered hands. He was feeding her, caring for her.

When the food was all gone, Daniel taking plenty of food for himself, he poured them both a coffee. He folded up the newspaper throwing it away from him.

"Here is your coffee. This is too hot, and I don't want to risk burning you." He handed her the cup. She took it and swallowed some down.

He kept watching her.

Should she say something?

"Thank you, Sir."

"Dawn?"

"Yes, Sir?"

"Did you feel how hot the coffee was?" he asked.

His face was a blank mask. She didn't know why he was asking such questions. Staring into the coffee cup, she frowned. Steam was rising from the cup. She'd always been able to drink hot liquid. Being a wolf she was able to heal a lot faster than humans.

"Erm, no. It tasted fine, why? Is there something wrong, Sir?" she asked.

"No, nothing is wrong." He gave her a quick smile before getting to his feet. With his back to her she stuck her finger into the hot liquid. There was no pain. The wolf inside her was growling at her. When she withdrew her finger she saw the scald, and yet she'd not felt anything.

You've not felt anything in a long time. This is

what you've been hunting for, the ability to feel pain.

Her wolf was pacing, clearly distressed. She placed her hand on her lap watching her skin begin to heal.

"Have you ever been in a fight?" Daniel asked, washing the dishes.

"Not really. I've seen fights but never been in one."

He wiped his hands on the towel and turned to face her. "Why did you dip your finger into the cup?" he asked.

She gasped. "How did you know?" she asked.

"The scent of burning flesh, Dawn. You tested the liquid with your finger. It's not completely burnt, yet you had a scald that has now disappeared. Tell me why you didn't call or scream."

"I'm a wolf. My pain is different from others'."

"Wolves scream at burns, broken bones, even the pain from the way I bit you last night."

She swallowed around the lump in her throat.

"I don't know why," she said, rubbing her hands down her thighs. "I really don't know why, Sir."

Staring down at her finger, she was curious as to why she didn't call out. Her lack of attention had brought her secret to his attention.

It's because you crave pain that you can't feel. You're sick, twisted, and need to feel pain.

Tears filled Dawn's eyes as she looked up at Daniel. "Do I repulse you?"

Chapter Six

Going to his knees before her, Daniel stared into her eyes seeing the fear shining within her depths. How long had she been hiding this inability to feel pain? Congenital Analgesia was very rare in wolves, but Daniel had heard of certain cases where wolves were tormented or physically abused during their transition. Around a wolf's eighteenth birthday they went through the transition that rewired their brain to connect to their wolves. The problem with this condition was in wolves it was harder to treat. He stared down at her finger seeing it had already healed.

Wolves hid it away, and he understood why as he'd also heard of packs using wolves with Congenital Analgesia to fight to the death. They didn't need to stop even with broken bones as they didn't feel it. Cupping Dawn's head, he tilted her head back and slammed his lips down on hers. There was so much going on in that head of hers that he didn't have the first clue where to start. For the last year she'd been hiding this from him. Had she been hunting pain in the hope of finding it? He should have seen it. Whenever he spanked her, she'd made all the right noises, but it was lies.

Sliding his tongue along her lips, he plundered her mouth tasting her.

His wolf pounced wanting out, to mark his woman and to prove to her they didn't hate her. They were in love with her.

Down.

No, we have to claim her. She's hurting. We need to prove to her it doesn't matter. She needs us.

Not now.

Dawn needed them to be stable around her. He withdrew, dropping a kiss on her nose. "Baby, I'm never repulsed by you. I'm curious about what's happened in your life."

"Surely you can't feel too much of a burn."

He licked his lips, wondering what to say. "No, Dawn. I can't stick my finger into steaming coffee without it hurting. Last night, I bit down on your nipples pretty hard. Did you feel it?" he asked.

"It was nice. My breasts are sensitive."

Daniel moved his hands down to cup her breasts. He saw the outline of the bruises. On her dark skin it was harder to see the bruises, but they were there. He ran a thumb over the tips, and she gasped.

"Sensitive, Sir," she said.

Nodding, Daniel sat back and stared at her body. He needed to talk with a professional, and the only person he knew was a doctor.

"Go into the sitting room. I'm going to finish cleaning the dishes. I want you to kneel beside the coffee table and present to me." She got to her feet, and he caught her wrist before she could leave. "This is not a punishment, Dawn." He pressed her hand to his cock. "I want you. I'm not repulsed by you, but I'm concerned like any other mate would be."

"There's nothing to be concerned about, Sir." She dropped her head showing her submission.

"Let me be the judge of that." He placed a kiss to her head, inhaling her scent.

Daniel watched her leave, pulling out his cell phone. He left the house, going out the door that led into the garden. Dialing Jake's number, he waited for his friend to answer his call.

"Hello," Jake said, groaning.

"It's nearly eight. Why are you still in bed?"

"Well, my alpha kicked my ass out of the house and I don't need to worry about getting up early."

He laughed. "I need you to get the Doc here."

"What did you do?" Jake asked. All the sounds of sleep disappeared from his voice. "Are you okay?"

"I'm fine." He looked through the kitchen. "Dawn's not okay, and no, I didn't do anything. I think something happened to her during the transition."

"What?"

"Dawn can't feel pain."

"How is that possible?" Jake asked. "You've been spanking her for the last year. Surely you would have seen something by now."

He heard sounds over the line and imagined his friend moving around. "I missed this. I don't know how it happened, but I gave her a coffee this morning. It was steaming, Jake, and she drank it down as if it was cold. When I asked her about it she told me she always drank hot liquids."

"That's not so strange."

"She put her finger inside the cup. Her skin burned, and not a sound came from her. She looked like she'd put it in body temperature water. Also, last night, I caused a lot of pain, and she only gasped and cried out. Not once were any of her moans coming from the ability to feel pain. She also doesn't look shocked by her lack of pain. Dawn is scared of me being repulsed by her."

"Alpha, this is bad."

"I know it's bad, but I need you to get the Doc here and to make sure no one knows the truth."

Jake was silent.

"What do you want to tell me?" Daniel asked.

"I heard some guys talking at the club last night. They were talking about some kind of dog fight or some shit. There's a guy who can't feel pain and is taking on dogs in the ring. I don't know if it was true or if they were bullshitting. Do you think it can be a wolf with this same problem?"

Daniel cursed. "I don't know. I really don't know. I'm not having anyone putting Dawn in danger because she can't feel. Check out the gossip and get back to me. In the meantime, get the Doc here. I want him to talk to him and see what I can find out."

"What if she can't be fixed?" Jake asked.

"I don't need her to be fixed. I just need to keep her safe."

Jake hung up letting him know that he wouldn't talk about Dawn's problem. Entering the house, Daniel placed the phone back on the kitchen counter. He ran his fingers through his hair trying to focus on Dawn rather than the fear of what her condition could mean. If she was trying to find someone to give her pain then she could have encountered all kinds of sick fucks. There were men, like him, who liked to cause a little pain, sadists, but they trained hard not to push too hard.

Some men and women, however, didn't care how much they pushed. They didn't believe in any boundary and simply pushed.

In her quest to find a sadist had she found this kind of men?

The very thought sickened him. Something had happened to her, but he didn't know what it was.

He walked toward the sitting room, finding her in the nearest one. She was kneeling on the floor with her dark thighs spread open for him to see the naked lips of her sex. Her head was bowed in submission. Daniel wanted to touch her body. Her dark skin called to him, leaving him in need to feel her, to taste.

"You please me, pet," he said, entering the room. He pushed the coffee table out of the way and circled her body. She released a little gasp as he moved the table with ease. Stroking her head, he stared at the curves of her body. She was perfect. He took a seat on the sofa. "Move to face me."

She shuffled on the floor, her head still bowed, but she settled between his thighs. Her naked, curvy body was on display for him to touch.

She's not ours yet.

He cupped her chin and forced her to look at him. "You can't feel pain, Dawn."

The change inside her was instant. He held her chin even as she made to pull away from him.

"You don't know that. It will happen soon."

"Sticking your finger into a steaming cup of liquid tells me all I need to know. You didn't make a sound. Last night, you didn't respond to my bites. I turned you on, but I didn't cause you pain."

"I like a lot of pain."

He stared at her, seeing the denial within her depths, and the lies spilling from her mouth.

"I don't know what you like to feel. If you can't feel pain then in certain cases, the person starts to feel like they need pain. You're not craving pain, Dawn. You're hunting for it because the idea of not feeling it scares you." She stared at him with tears in her eyes. He released her face and reached down to haul her up into his lap.

Dawn didn't fight him as he settled her onto his lap. He wrapped his arms around her body, holding her tight against him so she couldn't move.

"We're going to talk about this, and you're not going to argue with me." He infused his alpha voice as he spoke. She stopped struggling. The hairs on her arms stood on end letting him know he was winning their little dispute. He rested a hand on her stomach while the other he placed on her thigh. "Something happened during your transition. Most young wolves have a family or a pack that cares about them. They're nursed during their transition into their first turning. During that time the body goes through a lot of stuff. In rare cases, wires get crossed, and something bad happens." He was using all of his own knowledge to tell her this. The only reason he needed the doctor was for him to assess if there was anything they could do to stop the wires from being crossed. "These bad things turn an ordinary wolf into someone who can't process pain. When people find out about their lack of pain threshold it makes them vulnerable to predators." He licked his lips. "For you, you're a natural submissive, so you're open to men or women who'd want a toy to play with. They're sadists of the worst kind, Dawn."

He looked to her side and saw the tears glistening in her eyes. How much had she endured in the last few years before she met him? No one had looked deep enough to see the need she was suffering.

"Have you dealt with this?"

She gasped and turned her head away.

"Baby, I can't help you until you tell me the truth."

"How do you know I'm like this?" she asked, looking at him. "I didn't react to the liquid or to your bites, but why does it have to mean anything?"

"Because you're broken a little. Your wolf is scared to trust you." He rubbed circles against her stomach soothing her. "The only reason for your wolf to be scared is because you've put her in a situation that scares her. She doesn't trust your judgment, which makes her nervous. It's why you can't sense the truth of me being your mate." He kissed the side of her neck. "It's time for you to realize you can trust me." He pressed another kiss to her neck. "I'm here to stay, and no matter what you say, I'm always going to be here. I love you, and you're not getting rid of me." He held her tight against him, showing her the love and care he felt through touch.

"You're going to leave," she said.

"I'm not going to go anywhere. It's time for you to share these problems."

She didn't talk about her mother or any part of her past. How far back did this abuse go?

"Where do you want me to start?" she asked seconds later.

"From wherever you feel comfortable."

She stayed silent for several minutes, not talking. Her heart was racing, and her wolf was pacing in wait. *Calm down, baby. I'm not going to let her go.*

"I killed a human male and cleaned the mess up." The words were not what he expected and yet they were. She was a wolf, suitable to be his mate.

"Tell me what happened." He continued to stroke her body. "Why did you kill that man?"

"I liked pain, or I thought I liked pain. The guy I lost my virginity to he wasn't clean about it or nice. It hurt a little. I don't know if it hurt or if it was supposed to hurt."

"I get it," he said, kissing her shoulder.

"It was before my transition. I was eighteen, and I wanted to have sex as a human. I heard that some wolves couldn't have sex without turning. If I got a human mate I didn't want to risk killing him so I decided to have sex before. There was a little pain, but I didn't have an orgasm. That was the last time I ever felt pain."

He listened to her talk, finally opening up to him. Her wolf stopped pacing and simply rested, clearly happy that she was trusting someone with the truth.
****

"Afterward I thought I needed the pain to get off.

I couldn't enjoy sex any other way, and so I did a little research and I found people who felt the same. Before my transition, I could feel pain, and all of a sudden, it was gone. I figured I had to go looking for it." Dawn opened up telling Daniel everything about herself. She'd never thought telling the truth would make her feel safe, yet it did. "The first BDSM club I went to was for humans. There were no wolves present. In my father's pack, there's no relationship of this kind. I doubt they even know it exists."

"You'd be surprised what goes on behind closed doors, baby. It happens more than you think." He kept stroking her stomach and thigh, calming her.

Her wolf was relaxed, happy even.

"You went home with a man?" Daniel asked.

"Yes, he was the first man I went home with. I spent the weekend with him. He was…" She stopped thinking as the memory crashed over her. "I don't know his name. He was disgusting, filthy. He tied me to ropes he had coming from the ceiling and kept me that way for the time we were together." She closed her eyes, reaching down to touch Daniel. The feel of his flesh calmed her nerves.

"I'm here, Dawn. I'm not going anywhere."

Knowing he wasn't going to leave her filled her with joy.

"He used knives, whips, wax, and sometimes he used flame. There was no end to what he did. I made the noises suitable even though I felt nothing, and only when he started to talk about another woman he'd had in the same spot—" Her mouth went dry at the cruelty of his actions. "He'd killed another woman in that same spot. I hadn't smelled it because of all the scented candles and bleach he used to mop everything up. He talked how he'd tortured her for days, doing to me what he'd done to her."

"What happened?"

"My wolf pounced." She held her hand up for him to see. "My hand turned into the claws of a wolf. I tore the restraints with so much ease, and I killed him. I liked it, Daniel. He was a murdering bastard and had caused so much pain, and I liked causing him pain. I'm not normal."

He cupped her cheek, turning to her to look at him. His dark brown eyes stared back at her. "You saved other women. If you'd not been a wolf he'd have killed you and done it to other women."

"I spent three days cleaning up the mess and disposing of the body. For weeks afterwards I thought all I could smell was his blood. Every second I spent with my pack I thought they knew the truth. No one said anything, and after a little time passed I went out. Don't get me wrong. There were men who tried to give me what I wanted, but it always ended in rejection and disaster." She wiped the tears leaking from her eyes.

"How many people did you kill?" he asked.

"I only killed one man."

"The world is an awful place, Dawn. You've been unlucky to have encountered men who were bad, and didn't know how to handle your problem. We're not all like that." He caressed her body, soothing her.

"That's it. I heard about Kinkster's after my last failed relationship, and I met you."

"There's only one man on your list?" he asked.

"Yes, isn't that bad enough?" She sniffled, trying to wipe the tears away.

"It's bad, but it's not as bad as I thought. I don't know how you could have thought I'd be repulsed by you." He kept touching her. Her wolf relaxed, stretching out as if she needed to sleep.

"You don't believe in violence."

"I don't believe in violence being the only answer. It doesn't mean I've not struggled in my life before. Taking a life takes part of us with them, Dawn. The man you've taken, he's with you no matter what kind of scum he was."

"I want him to go away," she said.

"I can't make him go away." He turned her so she was sat on the sofa. "You've not talked about your mother. Everything you've told me wouldn't have affected your ability to feel pain. You had sex before your transition, and that made you believe you needed pain to get off. You've not talked about her mother or your transition."

Her mother was always off topic as far as she was concerned. "I don't want to talk about my mom."

Daniel stroked a finger across her lips. He settled between her thighs, pressing his body on top of hers. Her wolf moaned within her mind, bowing down to his presence. "How does your pack feel to having me as your mate?" she asked, changing the subject.

"You finally believe we're mates now?"

"I can't deny it. Not many men would put up with what I've put you through."

He smiled. "We're mates, and in time you're going to see how bonded we are." He leaned down, pressing his lips against hers.

She closed her eyes, whimpering as his lips touched hers. The instant shot of pleasure thrilled her.

"Open your eyes, pet. Your Master demands it."

Dawn did as he asked, staring into his brown eyes. "My pack wants me to be happy. Being around you, even with the blue balls you've given me, gives me pleasure." He rubbed his nose against hers then caressed down to inhale the scent of her neck. "Do you feel pleasure?"

"What do you mean?" She arched up to his touch, wanting to touch him.

"Last night, did you orgasm, or was that all a lie?" he asked.

"No, I feel pleasure. Last night was not a lie. I gave you everything that I am. I don't hide from physical feelings. I've tried to feel pain, searched for it, and I always come back disappointed." She wouldn't lie about experiencing her first true orgasm by her mate.

"So we know you can feel pleasure as much as the next person. That's good news, baby, really good news." He sucked on her earlobe, and she gasped as goosebumps erupted over her arms. The pleasure was sudden, shocking in the intensity. "The only problem is your inability to feel pain."

"Does it really matter?" she asked, missing the feel of his lips on hers.

"Yes, it matters. I don't want anyone to have you. You're all mine, and I'm a selfish bastard when I want something." He pushed some hair off her face. "Do you accept my claim?"

She stared into her eyes. Her wolf waited for her answer.

"Yes, I accept your claim."

"Then you know I'm going to have to meet your father and mother. They're going to want to know who I am."

"Do we have to talk about this?" she asked, hating the thought of him meeting her mother.

"I'm not going to push you. We're not leaving this house for some time. You're going to tell me the truth whether you like it or not."

"This isn't easy for me," she said, gritting her teeth. She couldn't move as he held her tightly, refusing to let her go.

"And you think this is easy for me? For one year you've denied me. I've known you were my mate, and you held me back. I'm not going to let you do it again." He leaned in and kissed her lips. "You're my mate, my submissive, and I'm going to lay my claim to you but only after I've met your family."

She didn't want him to meet her mother. Her mother was awful, vile even.

He thrust his pelvis against her core. "I think it's time for that grand tour." Daniel withdrew from her, and she couldn't stop the whimper from leaving her lips. He was torturing her on purpose, she was sure.

"I'm naked, Sir," she said.

"Good. I like seeing the beauty of my submissive. You're truly beautiful, Dawn." He took her hand within his.

He's ours as much as we're his.

"This is one of the sitting rooms." He picked up the remote and pointed it at the screen. "Ah, yes, this is the sports room. The television will only take sports, so no one can complain about what's on the television."

Daniel spent all morning taking her from room to room. She loved the age of the house. He'd kept a great deal of the original design and only changed the colors to make them lighter. The details were beautiful as were the patterns on the ceiling. They moved from room to room, and she was surprised he even had a cinema room. "There was a time when thirty people lived here. My father loved to have the pack around. Over time some of the pack died because of old age and moved away with their mates. I keep everything the same as I love having the pack around, too."

"It's strange not having a pack close by," she said.

"I know." He led the way upstairs toward the first floor where their bedrooms were. After seeing the seventh bedroom, Dawn decided she didn't need to see all of them. When they were at the attic she smelled the age lying in wait. "I've kept a great deal of memories in here." He led the way into the attic. Inside, Dawn was met by the history of the pack. Pictures of men and women in reserved poses met her. She smiled at the cribs as well. "I slept in this crib," he said, pressing on the side so the crib rocked.

"This place is amazing."

"You've not seen the best part, baby," he said, taking her hand and leading her away from the attic."

"Where are we going?" she asked.

He didn't speak as he led her to the kitchen. When he opened the door leading to the garden she froze. Being naked inside the house was different from going outside in the open.

"I can't go out there, Sir." She bowed her head so he'd see she didn't mean any disrespect.

"Dawn, we're over twenty miles from the nearest house. We're totally alone, and you don't need to worry about a thing." He tugged on her hand and wrapped the other around her. "Do you really think I'd let anyone else see you naked?" He took her mouth, plunging his tongue within.

She moaned, opening up to him.

"Do you trust me?" he asked.

Opening her eyes, which she'd closed during his kiss, she stared at him. "Yes."

"Good." He stepped out into the open. She followed him feeling the slight chill in the air.

"There's going to be a storm soon," she said.

"I know."

He led the way down the path, and when they got

to the stoned path, Daniel picked her up in his arms to carry her across.

She let out a squeal, shocked by his strength.

He's an alpha. Of course he can lift you.

"I don't feel pain, remember," she said, laughing.

"I know, but I don't want to watch you walking across the stones." He placed her back on her feet once they were on the grass. Daniel took the lead once again walking toward the edge of the water feature. The beauty of the water falling captured her attention. She wondered what it would be like to stand in the water and have it wash over her. Dawn didn't realize she'd said it out loud until Daniel spoke.

"Another time," he said, kissing her. He took her past some of the trees and turned left. She didn't have a clue where they were going, and she didn't care.

Through the cover of trees she saw the small cabin. Daniel walked up the steps, keeping her with him. He took out a key, unlocking the door for her to enter. Again, he flicked the light switch on, bringing light to the dark room. There were no windows, and the privacy was welcome. She rubbed the chill from her arms, even though the weather didn't bother her.

"This is my playroom. I guess it's a play cabin. This is where I train on the equipment. I never want to hurt my submissive."

"Have you brought a submissive here?" she asked, staring at the room similar to the one in Kinkster's. She never thought he'd have a playroom close to the house. Her pussy grew wet at the sight before her.

"Yes, I've brought submissives here. I never expected to find my mate. Since I've met you, there hasn't been any other woman for me." She turned around and saw him standing with his arms folded. Every time he folded his arms, she was drawn to the thickness of his arms. There was nothing timid or tame about him.

"There've been no other men for me either." She wasn't upset that he'd brought other women here. There was no reason for her to be jealous or angry. "Am I your exclusive submissive?" She was putting herself out there even with her problems.

Chapter Seven

"Yes, you're my only submissive, and you've been a little disobedient today," he said, stepping up close to her. She looked up at him and smiled. Her smile had his gut twisting. He couldn't lose her. She hadn't opened up about her mother, but she'd told him the truth about her past. Her wolf was happy with the admissions as well. It was a start for both of them.

In time, Daniel knew he could get her to trust him. Whatever her concern was about her mother, he knew it was possibly the cause of her problem. Female wolves were supposed to be maternal, caring for their young. The way Dawn reacted, he doubted she was ever comforted by her mother. The way she reacted to him combing her hair this morning was another clue. She'd stayed perfectly still, obviously loving the feel of his fingers running through her hair. Did she know how she'd moaned and when he took a little time between strokes, she'd whimpered as if he left her? There was so much going on inside her head, and Daniel knew there was a lot of work ahead of him.

"Present to me," he said, watching her go to her knees, opening them wide for him to see her pussy. He took a seat in front of her, far enough away to see the lips of her sex glistening. She was truly beautiful. His dark, submissive beauty waiting for him to punish her.

His cock thickened, making it uncomfortable for him. He moved in his seat in an attempt to relieve the ache in his pants.

"Several times you addressed me without using my title." He stared around the room, wondering what he should do to tease her.

"I'm sorry, Sir," she said.

"Good, I don't need to hear your apologies.

You're going to be punished, but I believe you've been pushing me to use my hand on you." He ran a finger across his lip, curious as to what he should do. This was their first time truly alone with many toys at his disposal. In the club they may have seemed alone, but in truth, they were never alone. His pack would have come to her if she showed any signs of distress. They knew he had struggled not to claim her, and he'd asked Jake to interfere if it ever came down to it. Fortunately, it never happened as he'd always been in control. This time, he was in complete control of her, and she was at his mercy.

"What is your safe word?" he asked.

"Red."

"Good. Do not use it unless you wish the scene to end. You know how to get me to slow down, so I expect you to caution me when I'm going too far."

"Yes, Sir."

He doubted she'd ever use a caution or a safe word during a scene, and that alone concerned him. "I want you to get up and go to the bed. Lie down on your back and open your thighs wide."

She did as he instructed. He admired the rounded curves of her ass as she moved away from him. Fuck, she made him ache with need.

"Are you comfortable?" he asked.

"Yes, Sir."

Daniel moved to his display of toys. He had a selection of whips, canes, and paddles. He personally liked the cane. A long strip of leather with a small loop at the end was his favorite. He loved the sound of it as he brought it down on her flesh. The other tool he liked to use was his hand. The sting of his palm let him know that he was punishing his submissive properly. The last thing he needed was for his submissive to believe he was getting weak.

He decided to take the cane, a set of nipple clamps, and a brand new dildo. After he brought new submissives to his room he always made sure to use new equipment.

Placing the devices within easy reach he knelt down in front of her. He took hold of one of her ankles and picked up the silk tie connected to the post of the bed. Securing the silk around her ankle, he made sure it was tight enough to keep her secure but not so tight that it would damage her skin. There was no need to worry about pain with her, but he would always be cautious. Once he was happy with the first ankle he did the same to the second.

Kneeling back, he admired her flesh against the red silk. *Perfection.*

"Bring your head forward." She did as he asked, and he drew the length of her hair above her head. He secured the length with a clip he kept in his pants pocket. The strands were all out of his way exposing her sweet neck. "Beautiful." He cupped the back of her neck, tilting her head back. Claiming her lips, he slid his tongue into her open mouth. Her taste was amazing, and he could spend the whole day kissing her.

The mating heat began to build inside him, and he moaned as a fresh wave of pleasure struck him. His cock hurt him with how swollen he'd gotten.

Leaving the kiss, he glided his hand down to circle one hard nipple. Once again he went to his knees, bringing the clamps within easy reach. He didn't speak as he stared at the heavy weight of her tits with the brown tips of her nipples. Daniel was lost when he stared at her. She was exquisite. He didn't know how any man could have hurt her.

Our mate. We can protect and help her.

Daniel was never going to turn his back on his

woman. If he couldn't help her with her inability to feel pain, he'd spend the rest of his life protecting her. He'd find other wolves with the same problem to see how they coped.

He sucked one of her nipples into his mouth, moaning as the hard bud filled his mouth. Opening the clamp he pulled away to see her nipple rock hard. He secured the clamp onto her nipple, and she gasped.

"How does it feel, pet?" he asked.

"It feels amazing. I've never…" She released a groan as he teased her clit.

"No pain?"

"No pain but it feels nice." Her sensors accepted pleasure, yet they denied pain.

Moving onto the next nipple, he did the same, relishing the sound of her gasp as he secured the clamp. She arched up against him, begging for more without saying a word.

"Lie back," he said. She lowered down to the bed. Her chest heaved with her indrawn breathes. Daniel got to his feet and found the silk binds to secure her wrists. He caught her gaze with his own. Her eyes were wide as she looked back at him. Neither of them spoke a word as he placed the silk around her wrist. He moved onto the next wrist and secured the last. There was no need for him to tighten the restraints as he wanted her at the end of the bed within easy reach.

He knelt between her thighs, grabbing the cane along with the dildo he'd brought with him. She stayed still, and he ran his hands up and down her body, watching her shudder and shake from his touch.

Her wolf was lax waiting for him to make his next move. Daniel smiled. He was more than prepared to take Dawn and her wolf. Under his care she'd flourish like the amazing beauty she was.

Opening her thighs, he stared at her creamy cunt feeling his mouth water for a taste of her. Her wet cunt was on display waiting for his toys. Closing the distance between them, he sealed his lips over her cunt sucking on the nub.

She cried out, jerking on the restraints. He slapped her thigh, glaring at her. "I told you to stay lying down."

Dawn went back to the bed, her body shaking as he went back to sucking on her clit. She continued to moan, and her legs shook beneath his. He gripped her thigh hard, adding to the sensation he was creating. She couldn't feel pain yet she could feel his touch, and he intended to use it all to his advantage. There wasn't enough touch between them to bring her to orgasm. He continued to grip her thigh repeatedly in different areas, constantly touching and stroking her.

Cream spilled from her pussy, coating his mouth, and he drank her up.

Reaching for the dildo, he replaced his tongue with the fake cock. He ran the tip of the fake cock through her slit coating it with her cream. Once the dildo was covered he worked the tip down to her cunt. Picking up the cane, he watched her response. Dawn was staring at the plain ceiling. He wondered if she liked the mirror above her bed or if she hated it.

Pushing the cock into her pussy he brought the cane down onto her leg. She cried out, and he did it again working the cane on her thighs. He didn't go anywhere near her pussy or body. Daniel watched her responses, cautious in his hits. The clamps were biting down on her nipples but not drawing any blood, each item creating a different sensation that wasn't pain, but it was something.

When she was at the peak about to fall into

orgasm, he withdrew the fake cock and stepped away from her.

"Sit up," he said, kneeling back on the floor. He removed one clamp then the other, paying careful attention to each bite. Daniel sucked on the flesh of her nipples, cautious in his ministrations. The clamps had been on her body for some time. Satisfied that he hadn't broken the skin, he took the toys toward the sink.

He sensed her confusion, and he smiled. Didn't she realize there were sweeter, easier ways to punish her rather than to cause her immense pain? There was no punishment in trying to cause her pain. She couldn't feel it.

Washing the toys in anti-bacterial soap, he dried them and placed them back in their place. He released her from the binds that kept her to the bed.

"Sir, have I done anything to upset you?" she asked.

Kissing her head, he leaned in close to her ear. "It's your punishment, Dawn. You're not going to be coming for the rest of the day, but that's not going to stop me from touching or playing with you."

She stayed on the floor in her submissive pose while he grabbed the bed sheets. Part of him didn't want to leave the room while another knew he needed to prove to her how far he could go.

His cell phone buzzed in his pocket. Taking the device out he saw a text was left from Jake.

Jake: Doc's here. He wants to see you. I'm at the gate.

"We've got to head back home." He waited for her to get to her feet, and he wrapped the blanket around her body.

"Have I upset you, Sir?" she asked. Her lip wobbled as he secured the blanket around her.

"You've not upset me. I'm giving you some much needed privacy. I've got a friend waiting at the gate. I promised you that no one but me will see you naked, and I intend to deliver." He took her hand. "The moment they're gone I'll be having you naked once again."

Daniel led her back to the house. He smelled Jake on the air, and he noticed Dawn smelled the air as well.

"You've brought the Doc here?"

"How do you know the Doc?" he asked, letting her lack of address slip. She was worried. Her wolf started to pace a little unsure about what was happening.

"He visited a wolf in distress during pregnancy." Dawn stopped in the garden. "Why's he here?"

"I've brought him here to see me. He won't know it's you."

"He will. How can you cover my scent? Shit, he can probably already smell me."

Daniel tightened his hand on hers, holding her tightly. "Pet, look at me. Look into my eyes." He waited for her to pause before he continued. "I'll never let anything happen to you. If your pack finds out we'll know who told. Don't worry, I promise your secret is more than safe." He pressed a kiss to her lips.

"Okay."

"There's no reason for you to leave. Come on, we'll go and meet the Doc together."
****

Dawn's wolf paced as they made their way around the front of the house. The blanket pooled around her legs, and she gripped the bottom so she didn't trip up or fall over. Daniel didn't move too fast, so she was able to keep up with each of his steps.

It took several minutes of walking before the gate came into view. She recognized Doc immediately. The other man she remembered from the club but didn't know who he was.

"Hello, Jake," Daniel said.

"Are we interrupting?" Jake asked, looking at her. She smelled Daniel on the other man, and she knew he was part of the pack.

"No." Daniel went to the electric box, opened the door, and typed in a code. The gates opened up letting the two men inside.

"Dawn." The Doc nodded his head at her.

Daniel stepped beside her, wrapping an arm around her shoulders. "Her presence here is to remain a secret," Daniel said, coming to her rescue.

She dropped her head feeling ashamed that she had to hide who she was from her family and her pack.

"I won't say anything."

Her mate stepped closer invading Doc's space. "I mean it. Anyone says anything and I'll be coming back for you."

Doc swallowed. "I didn't think you believed in violence?"

"I don't believe in violence, but if I'm pushed, I'll do whatever the hell I have to in order to protect my woman." Daniel stood to his full height, the scent of his wolf coming to the fore for all of them to know he meant business.

Goosebumps erupted on her arms as heat flooded her pussy at the dominant display.

"I've got it," Doc said.

"You're going to go all alpha on a woman who's denied your claiming?" Jake took a step closer. The anger rolled off him along with his disapproval.

She gasped at the smells coming her way along with the anger. Daniel growled, stepping in front of her.

"Daniel, you can do much better."

"She's my mate, Jake. You'll show her some motherfucking respect or I'll make sure you regret any words that come out of your mouth."

Jake stared at her, shaking his head. "He doesn't deserve you."

"I've accepted his claim," Dawn said.

"There's a reason she's accepted my offer, Jake. Come inside, and I'll let you listen."

Together they walked into the house. She noticed Daniel made the two men walk in front of them.

"Thank you," she said, resting against him. One of his arms wrapped around her back, holding her up.

"No need to thank me, baby. You're my mate and my sub. I'll take care of you for the rest of our lives."

She closed her eyes, relishing the feel of him holding her. They'd not even had sex, and yet she felt close to him.

Sex doesn't mean love.

The way he'd brought her to the edge of orgasm and yet denied her had angered and excited her. He was the first man to show so much control. Daniel turned her on by his masculine display.

They entered the house, going toward the sitting room that Daniel told her was only allowed to hold guests. He rarely let anyone further into his house who was not part of the pack. Daniel's pack may be different from many others, but his determination to keep them safe was that of a good leader.

She liked the thought of having the house filled with a loving, loyal pack.

"I want to thank you for coming," Daniel said, standing behind her as she sat down on the sofa.

Get closer.

Dawn moved into the sofa and snuggled up against his arm. Daniel seemed to know what she needed as he rested both of his hands on her shoulders, holding her.

"No problem. I don't see any problem, but I guess this is not a social call?" Doc asked.

"This isn't a social call." Daniel squeezed her shoulder. "Have you heard of other wolves who suffer with a condition similar to Congenital Analgesia?"

Doc frowned. "The condition is very uncommon in humans let alone in wolves."

"I've heard of it," Jake said. His arms were folded over his chest, staring at them. "The rumors were true. There's a wolf being used for sport." Jake glanced at her. "I've not been able to find him though. It has been a very busy morning."

She had so many questions.

"Is there any way to treat it?"

"What is this all about? I don't see what the problem is," Doc said. He looked between the two. She looked up at her mate, and Daniel stared back at her, waiting. Dawn nodded for him to tell the truth.

"Dawn can't feel pain," Daniel said.

"This is bullshit, Daniel. How do you know she's not lying to get away from you? She's been playing you from day one."

Daniel's wolf tensed. She felt him get ready to strike, and Dawn didn't want to be the one responsible for two pack males attacking. Getting up from the sofa, she opened the Doc's medical kit and withdrew a scalpel. Opening her arm, she slid the knife across her flesh. She didn't wince or feel the bite of pain. It was like her brain was cut off from feeling anything but pleasure. She felt Daniel's touch, the stings of the cane or his slaps. They didn't hurt her, and yet this kind of pain didn't have any affect.

She ran the blade across her arm twice more.

Dawn hadn't pressed the blade too deep, and the wounds started to heal seconds later. The first man she'd killed had pressed the blade in deep making it hard for her to heal.

"That's enough, Dawn," Daniel said. His voice commanded her to stop, and she stared at him. The concern was clear in his eyes. She handed the Doc back his scalpel and took her seat beside Daniel.

He covered the marks on her arms. Blood oozed between his fingers until finally the blood disappeared. Licking her lips, she stared up at him.

"Wait, you just took a scalpel to yourself," Jake said.

"This is not good," Doc said, moving forward.

Daniel growled, covering her with his arms. "I suggest if you intend to harm her you think again. I won't have anyone harming my woman."

"I'm not going to harm her." Doc held his hands up in surrender. "I'm only going to inspect her arms."

Several seconds passed before Daniel relented and allowed Doc to get closer. She held her arm out for him to inspect. There were no visible wounds.

"How long has it been like this?" he asked.

She swallowed past the lump in her throat. "Ever since my transition." It wasn't a lie as she'd felt plenty of pain before then. There used to be a lot of pain, and over time she stopped reacting to the pain inflicted upon her. After her transition, the pain no longer mattered. Her mother wouldn't leave her alone long enough to stop.

"There's no way for us to diagnose it unless we made our wolves vulnerable to the humans. In very rare cases something gets shut off during the transition in the emotional receptors of the brain. The reason I say very rare cases is the majority of the condition in wolves is based around abuse. The lines get switched, and the wolf can't decipher pain." Doc released her arm and looked at her.

She stared into his eyes, wondering if he knew the truth about her mother.

"Someone in your family, Dawn, has to be responsible for this."

"You mean, you can't feel anything?" Jake asked, coming closer. "Broken bones, boiling water, you can't feel it?"

Dawn shook her head, feeling like a freak show for them all to view.

"No, I can't feel it."

"Who did this, Dawn?" Doc asked.

"Is there a cure for this?" Dawn asked, ignoring his question. The conversation about the person responsible for her condition needed to be had with Daniel in private, not in front of these men she didn't know.

"I don't know. I've never met anyone with this condition." Doc ran fingers through his hair, obviously completely baffled. "This is dangerous, Daniel. If anyone found out about her condition, she could be used in unspeakable things. You've got to keep her safe."

Daniel's jaw tightened.

"What about the mating?" Dawn asked, turning back to look at the Doc. She couldn't live the rest of her life wondering if there was a cure.

"What do you mean?" Jake spoke up.

"If the transition rewired my brain then shouldn't the mating help me to rewire it again?"

Doc held his hands up. "I really don't know. I'm not going to say there's a cure, and I'm not going to say there isn't. I really don't know. There's a lot about this disease within wolves that we don't know. I can't help you with this."

"So you're pretty much no use at all?" Daniel asked.

"The mating is worth a try. Personally, I'd try to find fellow wolves in a similar situation as yourself." Doc stood, grabbing his bag. "Your secret is safe with me. This is not going to be good for other wolves if it's found out."

Seconds later Doc left the property.

"What are you thinking?" she asked.

Daniel moved around the sofa, tugging her onto his lap. "I don't like his lack of knowledge, and yet we call him a doctor. What I also want to know is where others are."

He stroked her thigh.

She snuggled in against him, pressing her palm against his heart. Daniel surrounded her with warmth.

"What if the mating helps?" she asked.

"I don't know, Dawn. I don't want to put you at unnecessary risk. I'd never change you." He kissed the top of her head.

Opening her eyes, she stared at his chest. In the past year Daniel had shown her more love and affection than the woman she called a mother had in her whole life. They hadn't slept together, and yet he left her feeling completely whole.

Tucking some hair behind her ear, Dawn spilled the truth out for him to hear.

"It was my mom," she said.

"What, baby?"

"My mom, she was always mean growing up, but she'd hide it away from Dad. He never knew the kind of woman he married and mated. She's not a true alpha, wasn't born one." Her chest tightened as she thought of the years she'd spent afraid of the one woman she should have trusted. "They're not a true mated couple. She was the one who caught his eye, and they had me." She stared up at him.

"You never talk about your mother."

"Because she doesn't deserve the title of mother." Tears spilled from her eyes, and she hated them. "When I was younger she used to hit me if I got my dress dirty or find ways to punish me. I couldn't do anything right, and she would tell me how useless I was. She'd lash out, slapping, hitting me, or scaring me. All the time she did, Daddy wasn't in the house. I noticed from a young age that she was always nicer to me when he was around. I tried to make him stay around a lot more, but he had pack work to deal with. I don't think he loved my mother. He cared about her, and he loved me, but she wasn't a true mate." Her throat felt dry as she started to tell him her memories. The memories she kept buried. "Where most kids went to their mother or pack female for help, I hid from her. She was a vicious woman."

Daniel held her tightly, and she was able to talk about all the bad memories she kept locked up inside.

"How does your father not see it?" Daniel asked.

"I don't know. Mom deals with the rest of the pack problems while he makes sure no one threatens the pack." She kept wiping away the tears, feeling the cleansing within her soul. No one knew of what she went through. This was the truth she'd given to Daniel, her mate, no one else.

"I'm not going to let this stand," he said.

"You can't do anything, Daniel. If you challenge my mom then you challenge my father first. He'll never let her accept a challenge she can't win."

"What do you think he's going to do when he finds out the truth?"

She bit her lip. "Nothing."

"These people you call parents suck. You're my

mate, and when the time comes I won't stand for anyone to hurt you." He kissed the top of her head, but fortunately, he let it go.

Dawn closed her eyes, snuggling in deep against him, loving the feel of his warmth surround her. There was nothing she wanted more than to be around her mate.

Chapter Eight

Several days passed, and Daniel took the time to gain more of Dawn's trust. He taught her the value of herself, and punished her when she pushed him a little too far. She begged for him to take her back to his cabin within the woods where all of his toys were. He had a selection within his room but not as extensive as the ones back at the cabin. Jake called him regularly to ask for updates. The pack was getting worried, but they were also sensing a change inside him.

He knew it was only going to be a matter of days before he claimed her. The full moon was tonight, but he wanted the chance to run wild with her. They hadn't had sex yet either. Their time together was through touching. He loved the feel of her hands on his skin. She drove him crazy with need. Yesterday he had used rope on her gorgeous body, tying the cords around her breasts and looping them through her legs to keep her bound up. He'd laid her on the coffee table, while he simply admired the view at the same time as stroking his length. She didn't complain about her position on the table or what he was doing. Her eyes closed at different intervals, and he saw the pleasure shining in her face. She was happy, and he couldn't find a single reason to protest.

When he could no longer stand to simply stare at her beautiful bound body he'd gone to his knees before her and enjoyed the taste of her pussy. He tortured her for over an hour, licking her delicious cream and taking his time to explore her clit. She was so responsive, and the rope helped to arouse her further by holding her down, adding to her pleasure. Only when he was ready for her to come did he give his permission.

He'd flicked her clit until she cried out in bliss, and he'd swallowed down every drop of her release.

Afterwards, he'd untied the rope and she'd gone into her submissive pose and begged for him to allow her to help him with his problem.

His cock had been rock hard and aching for release. Daniel had had every intention of going to the bathroom to relieve the ache. Instead, he'd sat down on the sofa and peeled away his jeans. His cock had sprung up as if it had a life of its own.

Seeing the yearning in her brown eyes, and the way she'd licked her lips was his undoing. There was no way a Dom could deny a sub who'd been a very good girl. She'd taken his cock within her mouth, sliding her tongue along the vein before going back to the head. Dawn had swallowed him down until he hit her throat, going deeper still. She'd bobbed her head while sucking on the root.

The feel of her mouth wrapped around his cock had been pure torture but of the most delightful kind.

Throughout her sucking, she'd stared at him, watching his reactions. He'd simply stared back, showing her how much he loved her lips on his cock. She'd surprised him further when she swallowed the cum that he erupted into her mouth. Afterward, he'd tugged her into his lap and held her while they watched a movie.

She hadn't worn any clothes since she came to him. Daniel was finding it harder to be around her and not to be inside her. He typed on the keyboard within his office, answering emails that had been sent to him in the past couple of days. The club, Kinkster's, still needed his attention as did his pack. Dawn knelt on the floor by the sofa with the book on the furniture as she read. Her hands were folded underneath her breasts, and she leaned on her arms as she read. Her feet were crossed behind her, moving from side to side as the rest of her body moved to whatever tune was playing in her mind.

He found himself constantly distracted by her movements. The emails were going unanswered while she was reading one of those sex books she'd found in one of the rooms. One of his wolves enjoyed some kinky books, which he didn't have a problem with Dawn reading. Anything that got his woman hot and horny was only a benefit to him.

She turned the page of the book and started reading again. The scent of her arousal filled the room, making it harder for him to concentrate on the latest email. He dealt with the financial problems of his pack. If some members wished to go to college, he footed the bill as they paid him back once they graduated and were in full time employment. One of the pack females was asking if she could go to medical school to train to be a doctor. He didn't see any concerns in helping her. A doctor within the pack could only help them all.

"You're doing that on purpose," he said, looking at Dawn as she turned to look at him.

"What?"

"The teasing with your body, moving and wriggling. It's distracting me." He sent her a smile, which she responded to.

She'd been completely engrossed into her book rather than seeing what she'd done to him. His cock was rock hard, wanting inside the wet heat of her.

"You're the one who keeps me naked, Sir," she said. "I wouldn't be that distracting if you let me wear clothes."

"Where would the fun be in that? I like you naked." He started typing away on his computer. Dawn closed her book and walked around the desk to rest against the hard wood.

"What are you doing?" she asked.

He reached out to stroke her naked hip. "One of

the girls who's just recently graduated from high school is asking for the funds to go to medical school after college. I'm responding for her to get her parents to come and see me with her."

"A nurse or doctor?"

"A doctor. The pack could do with a doctor of our own. There's not enough medical staff out there to deal with us." He finished typing the email arranging a date suitable.

"You're meeting her in a week at the local diner?" She covered his hand with her own.

"Yeah. You'll be coming with me. As my mate you're going to be helping me to build a healthier pack." He pressed send and watched the email go. Turning his attention back to his woman, he slid his hand up to cup her breast. "That is if you still agree to be my mate." He rubbed the tip of her nipple, watching her eyes dilate. Her wolf wanted to go out running, and she also wanted to fuck.

Daniel wouldn't be fucking his woman until he was ready.

"I want to be your mate more than anything." Her hands wrapped around his wrist, but she didn't try to stop him from touching her. With his other hand, he stroked the side of her body, loving the way goosebumps erupted along her flesh. He saw her stomach tense, and he pulled her in front of him.

It didn't take him long to have her sat on his desk with her legs wide open. "You're always spreading me open," she said, moaning.

He cupped her hot pussy, sliding a finger through her slit. "I'm always going to find a reason to have you spread open for my pleasure, baby. It's never going to change. You're just going to have to get used to it."

Daniel dropped his head, licking from the

entrance of her pussy up to her clit.

"No, Daniel, Sir, I need you inside me, please. I love your tongue, but I need to feel you." She tugged on his hair, stopping him from licking her.

Getting to his feet, he stared down into her eyes. "You want my cock inside you?" he asked.

"Yes, please, Sir, I need you." She ran her hands down the front of his shirt moving to his cock. He captured her hand stopping her from touching him.

He wanted inside her more than anything. Tugging his shirt over his head he threw the offending material away from him.

Dawn clawed at his jeans, tearing open the button trying to get the jeans free. He chuckled at her need for him. His wolf was ready to take her and claim her for his own.

Not yet. We'll claim her at the right time.

Wrapping his arm around her back he drew her closer and slammed his lips down on hers. She released his jeans, to grip his arms, moaning as he plundered her mouth with his tongue.

He moved down from her lips to her neck, sucking on the rapidly beating pulse. Daniel unbuttoned his jeans and shimmied them down his thighs. His cock stood out, long, hard, and proud. Fisting his length, he worked down her body to suck onto each nipple. Her fingers sank into his hair, pushing her chest out toward him.

"Please," she said, begging.

Daniel touched her pussy, pressing a finger deep into her core. She gripped him tightly, and he pushed a second finger within her. They both moaned as her pussy rippled around him.

He removed his finger, sucking the cream from it. "You taste so fucking good."

Gripping his shaft, he ran the tip through her slit, coating his cock with her cream. Only when he was satisfied that the length of him was coated did he slide to her entrance.

"This may sting a little," he said.

"I can't feel pain, remember?" She shot him a wicked smile.

Pushing only the tip of his cock within her, he placed his hands on her hips. "Still, you're going to feel full."

She licked her lips. Her tongue peeked out, begging to be sucked or bit.

"How do you know you're *that* big?" she asked. He smiled, and instead of answering her, he slammed to the hilt inside her, giving her all of him without letting up.

Dawn cried out, arching up as he penetrated her pussy. Staring down at where they were joined, he was amazed at how she opened up to take him. His cock filled her tiny pussy. Each ripple and pulse fluttered along his shaft.

He kissed her tits moving up to claim her mouth, which was open from the scream.

"Okay," she said. "I believe you're that big."

She was the first woman to take the full length of his cock without complaint. Staring down at his woman, his mate, Daniel was completely lost. She was his other half, the woman by his side, and they'd be strong together. He loved her with all of his heart and soul.

"You're mine," he said, laying his claim. He pressed a hand to her heart, feeling her beat. "I'm going to claim you, and the pack is going to accept you as my mate."

"Yes, Daniel. My Master."

He pulled out of her tight heat, watching his cock

appear slick with her cream. Daniel didn't get all the way out of her until he was slamming back inside, relishing her sweet screams.

"I'm going to fuck you so hard on this desk and then I'm going to fuck you all the way upstairs until we get to our bed. I'm going to love you for the rest of this day, and tonight, we're going to run together." He swiveled his hips, hitting the g-spot deep inside her.

Their cries mingled on the air as he took her hard on the desk. He sucked on her nipples before taking her lips with his.

"Touch me."

She gripped his arms tightly as he rode her body. He wrapped his arms around her body and picked her up. In the next second he had her pressed against the wall. Dawn held him tighter, and he took her lips, slamming his tongue into her mouth, matching the strokes of his cock in her pussy.

Being inside her was much better than he ever imagined.

****

Dawn held onto her mate, the love of her life, as he drove inside her. His thick cock filled her up, and there was no choice but for her to accept his loving. She kissed him back, meeting his tongue with her own.

For a year you've denied this.

She felt like an idiot for making them both wait. They were more explosive than she ever imagined. His nails sank into the flesh of her back, delighting her with the passion he was showing.

"So fucking close." He plunged inside her. She broke away from the kiss and rested her head against his neck. Dawn licked the flesh over his pulse as he rammed home, getting close to orgasm.

"Finger your clit, baby. I need you to come."

She reached between her thighs and stroked her clit, crying out at the instant shot of pleasure that struck her. Pinching her clit, she bit down on his neck wanting to mark his pale skin.

"That's it, baby, leave your mark on my skin." He rode her harder still. He stroked her clit as she felt the beginning of her orgasm start to build.

Releasing his neck, she threw her head back erupting onto his cock as her release crashed over her. Daniel growled, sealing his lips over her neck and biting down. He broke the skin and started to swallow down her blood.

His cum filled her pussy along with his mating heat. If any wolf was to get close to her now they'd smell Daniel all over her. She cried out as he took enough of her blood so he smelled like her. The start of their mating had just begun.

After several seconds passed, Daniel released the bite, licking the wounds as he retracted his canine teeth. She let out a sigh and rested her head on his chest, taking several deep breaths as she did.

"There's no stopping it now, baby. We're going to be together."

"I've got no problem with that. I don't think I can move," she said. Her head was swimming, and she moaned as her neck started to ache.

She pressed a hand to her neck groaning.

"What's the matter?" he asked, concern filling his voice.

"I don't know." She withdrew her hand to see some blood on her hands. Dawn frowned. "I think, I think it hurts." She rubbed the blood between her fingers before going back to cup her neck.

"What do you mean?"

Dawn winced as Daniel moved, and his cock

withdrew from her pussy.

"Ow!" Her pussy was tender but in a nice way. "I think I can feel pain."

He took a step back, staring at her as she looked up at him. Daniel lowered her to her feet, and she would have collapsed in a heap if he hadn't caught her.

"You can feel pain? What hurts?" He held her close to him and looked over her body, taking plenty of care as he touched her.

"My neck, it stings where you bit me, and my pussy is a little tender. Could it be the mating or something else?" she asked. Was the feeling temporary?

She didn't care if it was temporary or not. For the first time in over eleven years she felt something.

"The mating has started, and you're able to feel. If we complete the mating it could help with your ability to feel pain, not that you want to feel too much pain." Daniel lifted her up in his arms and carried her upstairs toward their bedroom.

"I thought we were going to fuck our way up to our room," she said, smiling.

"We'll fuck soon. I want to take care of you first. This is my right as your mate."

She wrapped her arms around his neck, holding onto him. "You know, you don't need to protect me from everything. I'm not that fragile."

He placed her on the bed and left her to go through to the bathroom. She felt his cum leaking out of and stood up before she made a mess of the bed. Daniel appeared several seconds later with steam coming out of the bathroom.

"Our bath awaits."

Again, he carried her through to the bathroom and eased her into the warm soapy water. He climbed in beside her, wrapping his arms around her body. She ended up in his lap with his flaccid cock resting between the cheeks of her ass.

"I think you're doing this on purpose," she said, leaning against him. His rock hard body met her back, surrounding her.

His arms, twice the size of hers, wrapped around her body securing her to him. "I love you, baby," he said.

She gasped, glancing toward him. "What?"

"You heard me. I'm in love with you and have been for a long time. I not only want you as my mate, Dawn, I want you as my wife." He cupped her cheek, turning her to look at him. "Tell me you'll marry me."

His proposal took her by surprise.

"You still want to marry me even knowing what you know about me?"

"Yes, baby. I want to marry you. Not only do I want to marry you but I also want you to have my children and grow old with me." He dropped a kiss to her nose. His thumb stroked her cheek.

"I love you, too." She smiled up at him. "I want to be your woman in every sense of the word." Dawn reached up to cup his cheek. "Kiss me."

He leaned down, and she moved up to meet him half way. When their lips locked, electricity ran up and down her body. She was drawn to him, and her wolf wanted out to have a taste.

She spun in his arms deepening the kiss. His hands held onto her back, and she opened her eyes to see their reflections in the mirror. They were beautiful, or at least she thought they were beautiful together. Her darker skin stood out against his pale skin. He was larger than she was, but together, the sight took her breath away.

Daniel pulled away.

"No, we're not going to fuck in the tub. I'm going to wash your body and then we'll fuck."

He wouldn't budge even as she cupped his rock hard cock. Daniel slapped her hands away, warning her of a severe punishment if she didn't listen to him. She enjoyed his attention and the way he bathed her.

The love he showed touched her deeply, and she never wanted it to end.

When he finished, he pulled out the plug and made her stand up.

He held a towel for her to step into.

"I love you, Sir."

"You're not getting my cock until I'm good and ready."

They walked into the bedroom together. Daniel dried his body, and the sight of his muscles rippling was enough to make her mouth water.

He dried her body when he was finished with his own.

"What's going on in that head of yours?" he asked, touching her body as he continued to use the towel.

"Nothing. I'm happy. It has been so long since I've been happy it just feels strange. I'm waiting for something bad to happen."

He caught her to him, pressing his forehead against hers. "I'll never let anything bad happen to you. You're not going back home without me, especially if you can feel pain again. You're mated now, and your father's got no excuse to keep you at him." Packs were more possessive of their children. Unless the children were mated, parents expected their children to stay close to home. Her mother couldn't get rid of her without her father knowing the truth.

"She won't harm me around my dad."

"Baby, you've already told me more than once that he's not always around. I'm not risking it. We'll go to your dad's soon."

Dawn wanted to go to her father right away with the news. She didn't want to dispute or argue with Daniel's claiming. The love she felt for him was consuming, soul deep, and that kind of love couldn't be pushed aside for anything. Once her mother saw that she had no more hold over her, everything would be over. Daniel was her Dom and Master.

"Do you want to meet all of the pack before we go to your father's or after?" he asked.

"Before. We need to know they're happy with you taking me as your mate."

"I wouldn't care what they thought, Dawn. I care about my pack, but you're my mate. I'm not going to let them decide for me." He squeezed her ass. "Now, before we go and get something to eat I'm going to be inside you again."

With his grip on her ass, he lifted her up and tossed her to the bed. She let out a little squeal, giggling as Daniel followed her down.

"Now, I wonder if I can have you screaming in pleasure in no time."

She opened her legs not prepared to argue with his skill.

Daniel skimmed his hands up the inside of her thighs to rest on her pussy. He slid a finger within her core, spreading the digits out to stretch her. Dawn moaned, loving the thickness of his fingers but wishing it was his cock instead. He moved from her cunt to stroke her clit.

She whimpered as the pleasure took her by surprise.

He'd brought her to orgasm less than half an hour ago, and already she was begging for a second. Daniel showed no signs of slowing down. His own orgasm of thirty minutes ago hadn't stopped him from getting hard once again.

"I'm going to fuck you hard and have you screaming my name." He spoke the words as a promise more than anything else.

"Please," she said, begging him. Daniel pinched her clit with his nails, and the pain was instant as was her arousal. She'd never felt something so amazing before in her life as the jolt of pain enhancing the pleasure he was creating with his fingers.

"You feel that?"

"Yes, don't stop please."

One of his hands left her leg, and the next second she felt his cock at her entrance. He eased the first inch within her as he pinched and tapped her clit.

"You're so fucking tight," he said, growling the words against her lips. He sucked her bottom lip into his mouth, biting on the flesh. Each little jolt of pain heightened her pleasure. "I can smell you, Dawn. You're so aroused, and you can feel the pain."

"Yes, it feels so good. Please, don't stop, Sir." She didn't mind begging so long as he never stopped what he was doing. Dawn didn't want this kind of pleasure to end.

He slammed within her and continued to pinch her clit. She closed her eyes, relishing each new sensation as he fucked and loved her body hard. She gripped his arms, wanting everything he had to offer.

Mates, lovers, marriage.

She was going to have it all with him. No more fear or worry when it came to her future and knowing that excited her. She thrust up to meet him, fucking his cock as he pounded inside her. He released her clit to grip her hips. There was nowhere else for her to go. She rode him as hard as he rode her.

The connection between their wolves opened up, and Dawn felt him. It was the strangest experience in her life but she felt Daniel, his wolf, his feelings.

"I've got you, baby. Do you feel that? Our wolves crave each other the same way we do. This is what was supposed to happen."

"Yes," she said, responding to his words. Their wolves were destined for each other. She felt it deep in her soul. Daniel wasn't only her mate, her Master, and the man she loved, he was her soul mate, the one born to match her in all things.

When their orgasms came, it was explosive. She wrapped her body around him, holding him tightly as their bodies pulsed together, awakened by their new connection for each other.

His cum filled her as she washed his cock with her own. Their minds mingled together, coming almost as one.

"What's happening?" she asked, feeling so much more from being with him.

"We're mating and bonding, baby. This is what it means to be a true alpha couple."

She'd found the one, and no matter what it took, Dawn was never going to let him go.

Chapter Nine

Daniel watched as Dawn blew across her coffee. They were going out for a run shortly, but she'd tried to swallow down the hot liquid he gave her. She'd screamed in pain and now was having to blow before sipping the steaming coffee. Their bond was helping to secure the feelings that had gotten lost during her transition.

"What did your mom do to you during your first transition?" he asked. He was sitting on the table beside her, resting his feet on the chair as he stared. "I know you don't want to remember those kinds of memories, but I think it will do you good."

She took another hesitant sip of her drink. "This is strange for me," she said. "I've never had to be overly cautious before. I like it."

He waited knowing it was taking her some time to compose herself.

"Dad was busy handling a pack dispute over some woman or something. I don't know exactly what, but he wasn't around. Mom made some excuse, and I was taken into the woods where our pack is close. All packs are near some areas that allow us to run freely."

The newly opened connection between them allowed him to sense the pain within her, the emotional pain she kept locked up when it came to her parent. "What happened?"

"Before the transition happened she ordered everyone to stay clear of the woods because I was going to be there. We were alone, and she chained me to a tree using thick silver chains. The pain was unlike anything I can remember. There were times I thought she hated me, and in that moment, I knew she did. She despised me because I posed a threat to her. I don't know how or even why I posed a threat, but she made sure I knew how much she hated me." She pushed some hair that had fallen off her face.

Anger spread throughout him imagining a young, terrified girl as she was going through her first transition.

"She kept me there, watching as my bones broke. There was no help or comfort. She watched, taunting me and my wolf, breaking me down. I don't know why she was so determined to make my wolf terrified of her."

"Did your mother win her role within the pack, or was it natural?" he asked.

"She fought to be the strongest female, and she trains daily to make sure no one can defeat her."

He rubbed his temples. "In rare cases a young wolf born to an alpha male and a strong female can inherit alpha traits that mean when she's fully transitioned, her wolf will fight to take her place as head alpha female or could even be voted to take the place as alpha female. In some packs, the alpha pair doesn't have to be mated."

"You think my mom was scared of this and so she scared my wolf to submission?"

"You're a natural submissive, but your wolf is strong. I've felt her even though she's been squashed for some time. I think your mother was determined to break your spirit from the start. It would be humiliating for her if her daughter had a natural higher rank within the pack." He wanted to hurt this woman, break her down and hurt her just like she'd hurt his woman.

"I wasn't allowed food or water. She beat me with chains as I transitioned. Each time my wolf appeared she'd beat me. It was like a constant punishment. If I didn't turn, she beat me, and once my wolf came out, she beat it. I didn't know what to do."

When he met this woman it was going to take all

of his strength not to kill her.

"Around day four of the transition my father was getting nervous. I sensed him close, but I couldn't beg him for help. I heard my mother consoling him, acting like the caring mother. When she came back, she knew it was over. I'd finally transitioned, and something snapped in my head. The chains she was using no longer hurt. She hit me, but it didn't hurt." Sweat dotted Dawn's forehead, and he used a clean towel to wipe her brow.

"Nothing is going to hurt you here, baby. I'm here, and I'm never letting another person come near you."

"I was scared of her, and I didn't say anything. My dad asked about the turning, and I stayed quiet. My mother would find times when I let my guard down and she'd hurt me, or at least believe she hurt me."

He tightened his hands into fists thinking of all the ways Dawn had been hurt.

"What was the worst?" he asked.

"Three years ago, I was making dinner for Dad, but he had to go out. She accused me of trying to take her spot, and she grabbed my arm. Before I could stop her, she forced my hand into the boiling water." Dawn smiled even as her eyes filled with tears. "I sickened her. She expected me to scream. I knew something was wrong as I didn't feel anything and yet my skin was growing tight. My mom backed off, and I withdrew my hand. It was red, scalded, but I was healing. I heal so quickly. I remember her asking me what the hell I was." He took hold of her hand, offering her comfort when she didn't need it. "I didn't respond, but I asked her what else she wanted to do to me seeing as I no longer felt anything she did."

"Stubborn even to a woman who could have hurt you." He cupped her cheek, caressing her with his thumb. "You've got to learn to take care of yourself."

"I didn't mean to say anything. The words slipped out, and the next thing I knew, she didn't want me at home. She made life uncomfortable but made sure none of the pack wanted to be around me. My father is so busy, and he doesn't see what's going on, but he told her I wasn't going anywhere until I was mated."

He couldn't bear to hear her say anything more. Wrapping his arms around her, he kissed the top of her head. "My pack will love you, and I promise you, you'll want for nothing."

"I love you, Daniel. I don't care about what the pack thinks."

The sun was setting outside, and he wanted her to see the beauty of his land. "Come on," he said, taking her hand. He led the way out to the night. They were both naked as they walked together.

They were going to face the world together, and the pack was going to love her. When he opened the connection he had with the pack, he sensed their curiosity about her. Jake was finally accepting her within their pack and had called him to voice his acceptance of his mate.

Daniel was proud of the pack he ran with. None of them knew the true pain Dawn had gone through to make it here. Staring at the sunset, he was more interested in looking at Dawn. Her brown hair was pulled up on top of her head.

"What are you thinking?" he asked.

"Your house is truly beautiful. This is a dream. I always had this dream growing up of something like this. Do you think it was fate, giving me hope to fight back?"

"I don't know what it is, but I'm so pleased you listened and didn't give in." He squeezed her hand a little tighter.

"I'll never give in. I'm a lot stronger than I look." She squeezed him back.

"Come on." He took the lead, walking toward the forest. The full moon was high in the sky, and the need to change was strong. He held it off, determined to ease Dawn into their first change together. "Do you want to do it in private?" he asked.

"No need. Turning into a wolf hasn't hurt me since that first time." She released his hand, standing away from him. He watched in amazement as her body changed and within seconds a black, cute wolf stared back at him.

Daniel didn't waste any time turning into his dark amber wolf.

"Nice," Dawn said, admiring him. *"I didn't think you'd be that big."*

"Baby, you've not seen anything yet."

She bumped him playfully before taking off for the forest.

"Alpha, I can feel her. She's strong." The thought came from Jake who was not far from the house. The pack was out in force, but he'd ordered them to stay away from the house. He was keeping Dawn close to the house, and he didn't want any of them scaring her. They were a new pack to her, and he wanted them in human form to meet her.

"She's far more than just strong. She's perfect, and she's going to be my mate."

"The pack is behind you. We'll protect her and you. We're all keeping our distance."

Daniel took off, following his woman deep into the forest. She was playing with him. He smelled her happiness on the air.

"I can hear you," he said.

"You can hear my thoughts, but can you find

me?"

"Are you challenging me, pet?"
"You're not my Dom here."
"I'm your alpha."
"Then catch me, alpha. Show me who's boss."
He ran through some trees knowing she was close. The scent of her intensified, getting stronger with every step he took.

"Got you." Dawn leapt at him, but he sensed where she was. He caught her, taking her to the floor beneath him.

"No, pet, I've got you like I've always got you." He licked her nuzzle.

"Ew, gross."

He chuckled and released her, watching her get to her feet. Together they ran around the forest, taking in the full moon together.

"I can feel your pack. I know they're here."

Daniel paused, staring at her.

"I don't mind. This is their forest. Are they happy I'm here?"

She couldn't sense their acceptance because she was part of another pack. When they finished their mating, she'd only be able to sense his own pack rather than her father's.

"Jake says so. I want you to meet the pack when you're ready."

"Then we should call them to meet us at the house tomorrow. I'd love to meet them to see if they'll accept me into their fold."

Daniel growled. *"They'll accept you because I fucking tell them to."*

"That's not how it works, and you know it."

He leapt into the air, catching her on the floor once again. Daniel turned back into a human as did

Dawn turned back as well. She was laughing at him. "You caught me again, Sir."

"You better believe it."

"So are we going to complete the mating today?" she asked.

The mark on her neck had faded a little. He wanted that mark to last for others to see his claim. The only way for that mark to stay was for her to lay her mark on his flesh at the same time. They were true mates, and all it would take was one time. Their mating would cause pain and pleasure, coming together in an explosion. The connection to her old pack would be severed, and the pack would feel Dawn as his woman, part of *his* pack.

"What if I can't feel pain anymore?" she asked.

"I don't care, Dawn. I'll have you feeling pain or not. You're perfect to me, and I love you with all my heart." He brought her hand to his chest. "It's never going to change and neither are my feelings for you. Are you ready to become my mate? Your father will feel you being torn from him."

She was silent for several seconds.

"Yes, I'm ready to become yours in all ways possible." She leaned up and kissed him.

"We'll have to deal with your father."

"I don't care, Daniel, so long as I'm with you and you remain my Master. I'm ready to move on and leave my old pack behind." Sitting up, he pulled her to straddle him.

She wrapped her legs around his waist, and he placed a hand to her back. His cock was ready to be inside her.

"You're the one in control," he said, leaving the claiming up to her.

****

Dawn gripped the base of his cock and slowly lowered herself over his rock hard length. She felt every inch of him sinking inside her, and she took her time to take all of him. Once every inch was inside her, she blew out a breath and stared into his eyes. The dark amber of his eyes flashed showing how close his wolf was to the surface.

"Be careful, baby, I'm holding on by a thread."

"Then hold on because I don't intend for this to last very long."

She squeezed his cock with her pussy walls, kissing his lips then sliding down to suck on his pulse. Daniel did the same to her, and they touched each other. The moon shone down through the clouds, shining on them. The power of the moon had goosebumps erupting over her flesh as she felt the claiming start to take over.

Her teeth turned, sharpening into canines. She sank her teeth into his neck tasting his blood flowing into her mouth.

Dawn cried out as he struck hard, sinking his teeth into her neck. The mating scent came from him, swirling around them as they drank and fucked. The hands at her back held her tighter.

The combination of pleasure and pain took over coming faster than ever before.

She closed her eyes trying to ride the pleasure as much as the pain.

"Hey, baby, I'm here."

The final link to Daniel's pack opened up. She felt the sudden excruciating pain as she was torn from her father's hold. Dawn felt her father wake up as she pulled away from him. She went willingly into Daniel's pack, feeling his love and warmth fill her where her father's pack never had.

He fucked her hard, and she retracted her teeth,

moaning as his cock filled her.

"I'm not going to last, baby."

"I don't care. Fuck me."

She reached down, stroking her clit as Daniel grunted. He released a howl out into the night, and his call was answered by several more. His pack had gained a new member, and in doing so, he'd gained a mate.

Their release mingled on the air. The pain of his mark along with the pleasure of his cum filled her.

"I can feel pain," she said, chuckling. Dawn collapsed against him, exhausted from the heat of the claiming.

"Your cell phone is going to be buzzing. Your father's not going to be happy I've taken you away."

She smiled against his chest. "I'm so happy. I've never been this happy before."

"Good, you're going to learn to be happier."

He stroked her back, and when he lay down, she went with him. His cock stayed still within her.

"I don't want to move from this spot."

"Neither do I." He cupped the back of her neck then glided down to grip her ass. "We're safe here until morning."

"You don't have any poachers?"

"No, I don't have anything that will put you at risk. Jake will take care of us."

"You're so sure of that?"

"Jake promised to take care of both of us. He's never backed down from a promise." He kissed her cheek. "I can't move right now. I never knew a mating would be like this."

"I can feel you, Daniel."

"And I can feel you. We'll deal with everything else in the morning. For now, I just want to hold and love you."

She kept her head on his chest staring at the forest floor. The smells and sounds comforted her. Time passed, and throughout it all, Daniel held her. They didn't speak as words were not necessary. Slowly, she felt her eyes begin to droop as sleep started to claim her.

The next thing Dawn knew it was light, and she opened her eyes to find a rabbit staring at her. She smiled at seeing the cute forest animal.

"I remember a time when rabbits would run away scared of me," Daniel said. His voice vibrated through her body.

"He's a cutie pie."

"If he doesn't move he's going to end up in a pie."

She jerked up and slapped at his chest. "Don't be rude." The action finally alarmed the rabbit, and he took off.

Smiling, Dawn looked down at her mate. Blood covered some of his chest from her bite. She'd not been the best marker. Glancing at the front of her body, she frowned. "Ew, I look like I've been a round with a vampire and lost." She looked a mess and hated to think what she looked like in the mirror. There were small bruises on her hips that hadn't disappeared.

"Our mating marks will last longer. The bite on your neck will remain permanently. The bruises will fade in a few hours."

"I don't care how long they last. I love having your mark on my body." Throughout the night his cock had slipped free of her pussy, but he was newly rock hard. "I think we can start the morning off well," she said, rubbing his nose with her own.

"I wouldn't," another man said, coming from the left. She frowned, trying to place his voice as she didn't recognize it.

"What is it, Jake?" Daniel asked, pulling her down to him.

"The pack is waiting to meet your mate. They're all at the house. Also, her cell phone has been going off throughout the night."

Her cell phone was tossed close to her on the forest floor.

She glanced at it, and it started to buzz. Picking the phone up, she flicked it open to see "Daddy calling" on the screen.

"I better answer this." She sat on his waist and accepted the call.

"I don't care what you say, Francie, I'm talking to her," her father said, talking to her mom.

"Hey, Dad," she said, staring into Daniel's eyes. He helped to ease her troubled thoughts.

"Honey, what the hell is going on? I can't feel you anymore. I don't understand what's going on?"

She tucked some hair behind her ear as Daniel took hold of her hand, stopping her.

"I've, erm, I've found my mate." She smiled down at Daniel, loving the fact she was mated. "His name is Daniel, and he's the man I've been staying with."

"What? You didn't tell me you were seeing anyone. Who is this Daniel?"

"He's probably some weakling, Don. Let her go." Her mother spoke up trying to be heard.

"Shut up." Her father growled at her mother. Dawn winced knowing her mother would find some excuse to blame her. "Dawn, what's going on?"

"Daniel's an alpha, Dad. We're mated, and we completed the mating last night. He really wants to meet you." She kept her palm over Daniel's heart, feeling it beat.

"He's an alpha?" her father asked.

She noticed her mother went silent.

"Yeah, he's perfect, and I love him."

Daniel took the phone from her. "This is Daniel. It's a pleasure to finally hear from you, Mr. Weldon. I've got some issues I want to talk to you about."

"Be careful how you talk to me, boy."

She listened as her father growled back at Daniel. It was strange hearing her father annoyed or arguing with another alpha. She was rarely around for his anger.

"We're going to meet. Dawn and I are coming to your pack this afternoon, and we're going to deal with shit I'm not happy about." Daniel pressed a finger to her lips to stop her from arguing with him. "Good, I'll see you there."

"Why did you do that? Daddy doesn't need to know what's going on."

"As far as I'm concerned, he needs to know. What if she's hurting other members of the pack? She kept you quiet, and you're the only daughter to the alpha. You don't know what she'll do next." He cupped her cheek then kissed her lips. "Come on, we've got to get out of here."

"I brought you some clothes. You both look like you stepped out of a horror movie." Clothes landed on the floor beside them. Jake sounded close by.

"You better keep your eyes to yourself," Daniel said, shouting toward his left.

"Don't worry. Your mate's dignity is still intact." Jake moved away from them.

Daniel helped her to her feet. She took his hands, going on her toes to kiss him.

"You're turning into a softie, baby. I don't even recognize my little submissive."

"She's still here, but she might not like a lot of

pain." She couldn't help but smile at her statement.

The weight of the world had been lifted off her shoulders all because of Daniel.

"I love you," he said. "I'll take you any way I can get you, and if that means I can only spank you three times instead of four then that's what I'll do." He cupped the back of her neck and tugged her close.

She loved his possessive display and the way he held her.

"Alpha, we're all waiting," Jake said.

Daniel pressed his head against hers. "We're going to have to go."

"Yeah and we can't even enjoy our time together seeing as you organized a meeting with my dad." She shook her head, pulling out of his arms to grab a shirt.

Dawn put the clothes over her body hating the feel of the clothes. It had been days since she last wore any clothes.

"You want to be naked, don't you?" Daniel asked, smirking.

"You did this on purpose."

"Baby, I'll do whatever it takes to get you naked and have you doing it willingly." He took her hand once they were dressed. "Let's go and see the rest of the pack."

Jake appeared through the trees looking tired.

"You stayed up all night?" she asked.

"Daniel wanted you protected, and I promised to do so." Jake walked beside them out toward the garden. Dawn gasped as she saw all of the cars parked within the grounds. She heard the sounds of the pack inside the house. How was this going to go well? Her mother despised her, her own father didn't see when she was in pain or not, and the only person who truly loved her was Daniel.

"What if they don't like me?" she asked.

"They'll like you, baby, because you make me happy." He stayed by her side as they both walked into the house. The pack all stopped what they were doing and started to converge on the main hall. She took several deep breaths, wishing there was some way to escape from this.

All eyes were on her and Daniel. He stood beside her, lifting up their joined hands for them all to see.

"I would like to introduce you all to my mate. This is Dawn, and she's part of our pack now. She's my mate, and any problems you have, you'll come to one of us. Do any of you have any concerns, questions, or desire to challenge?"

She tensed as he threw it out there for all of them to think about. Her palm grew sweaty as she looked at all the men and women. They truly scared the life out of her. If they all protested there was no way for her to fight them off.

"Actually, can anyone tell me where the sugar is? I can't eat my cereal without sugar. It's too gross."

"Yeah, where's the spaghetti sauce? We're all here and ready to get back to normal, alpha."

Many people started asking questions about something else.

Daniel chuckled. "Everything you need is either in the kitchen or the pantry." He rubbed her neck, and she groaned.

The pack started to move out of the room.

"Alpha, we're happy for you."

They were left alone. Even Jake had wandered off, leaving them.

"See, I told you. You're going to be loved here. Now, it's time for us to go and check out your pack." He kissed her cheek, taking hold of her hand and leading her upstairs. She went with him willingly.

Chapter Ten

Later that evening Daniel sat opposite Dawn's father and mother. He was struck by how cold the house was. Not only was the house cold but so was the pack. The chill filled the room, and it was all coming from one woman, her mother. He watched Don, her father, embrace her.

"Honey, I missed you, darling." He kissed her cheek, hugging her close. This man was so busy he didn't even see what was happening to his own pack. The excuse was pitiful at best. Dawn had been subjected to pain and torture because of her mother.

"Hey, Daddy," Dawn said, smiling.

She didn't look toward her mother, and neither did her father.

"You're all mated now. Wow, when did you grow up? It doesn't feel ten minutes ago since you were born." Don held her hand, the love shining from his eyes as he looked at her. "When I felt you being torn from me, I panicked. I've never experienced anything so awful."

"Don, please, she's a big girl. It's time to let her go. You should have let her go a long time ago," Francie said. Her mother was glaring at Dawn.

Daniel saw the anger, the fear, and the disgust within her mother's eyes. There was also envy along with jealousy. So many emotions coming from her mother but she wasn't a true alpha, as otherwise she'd have kept those emotions locked up tight.

"Stop it, Francie." Don glared at her, but the smile returned to his face when he looked at his daughter.

"You're always so busy with the pack, Daddy. You never really saw I was growing up."

"No, I didn't see a lot, did I? There are times I feel like I lost time with you, honey. I'm going to miss you." He turned to look at Daniel. "I don't suppose you'll let her visit me often, would you? I'm going to miss my baby."

Daniel tensed, seeing the glee in Francie's eyes. Yeah, he wasn't going to be letting his woman anywhere near this bitch.

"I can't allow her to come here unattended, Don. I'm sure you can understand seeing as her tormentor and abuser is still living here."

"Daniel!"

He held his hand up stopping Dawn from speaking.

"No, baby, you're not going to let her get away with this shit for much longer. I'm done and I can see he loves you very much, but I'm not going to let her get away with it."

Francie started to panic.

"What the hell are you talking about? My daughter has never been abused." Don growled the words, getting to his feet.

"Your wife, your mate, she's the reason your daughter has been unable to feel any kind of pain. She tortured her during her transition, keeping her chained to trees and beating her when she turned. Your mate tried to break my woman, and for that reason, I can't let her come here while you still have her." He pointed his finger at Francie.

"You can't do this!" Francie started to scream. "You little bitch. You couldn't keep your mouth fucking shut."

Her mother charged toward Dawn. His mate didn't move, twitch, or show any sign of fear. Before Francie got close, Don grabbed her around the waist.

"Is this true? Did you abuse our daughter?" He shook his wife, glaring down at her.

"She deserved it. The little bitch was always getting in to trouble and always running to you. She needed to know her place. This is not her pack. It's mine. Fucking mine."

"Her transition was her most important time. How could you hurt our child, our daughter? What the fuck is wrong with you?" Don's anger filled the room.

Daniel wondered if he knew what was going on in his own pack.

"She was just a way of getting you. You wouldn't have looked at me twice if I didn't get fucking pregnant. The only reason I've got you is because I was fucking pregnant." She spat the words back at Don. "This is my pack. Being your mate is my fucking right. She held alpha qualities. The moment you and the pack saw that, they'd have cast me aside. I wasn't going to let that happen. Bitch needed to be put in her place."

The bile coming from her sickened Daniel, and he had his answer. Dawn was a submissive, but she held the traits that only an alpha possessed.

"You're not my fucking mate." Don released her and stood. "All claim I have to you is over. I refuse to take a mate who can abuse my own daughter." Don turned to look at Dawn. "Is all of this true?"

"Yes," Dawn said, whispering the word.

"She's no daughter of mine. She's a fucking slut. I hate her. It's not fair. She doesn't deserve to have an alpha."

Suddenly, one woman entered the room. Daniel didn't have a clue who she was.

"I would like to make a formal complaint about your mate." The woman dropped her gaze. She was fidgeting with her hands.

Daniel watched in amazement as three more women he didn't know entered the room.

"The first woman is Leah. She cooks for us," Dawn said, whispering against his ear. Daniel didn't know what to make of it as he listened to several women speak against Francie.

Francie was cursing, trying to get to the women.

Don yelled out as he restrained his mate in his arms.

Daniel watched three men walk into the room.

"Take her to the basement. I want her locked in and make sure no one lets her out. I will not have any woman by my side who abuses her own daughter." Don's alpha power stripped Francie of her status, tearing her will from the pack. "We'll be talking with everyone in the pack. I know you were hard on the pack, and I want to know the extent of your supposed help. If you're lucky, you'll end up in jail, and if not, you'll be sent on the hunt."

The hunt was a pack's right to hunt the person who tortured them.

Dawn tightened her hold on his hand.

He turned to look at her. She didn't want to take part in any hunt or decision when it came to her mother.

The rest of the meeting with her father went by with him asking Dawn questions about what happened when she was younger. After a couple of hours Dawn took the lead and told him they had to leave.

Daniel promised to let Dawn visit with her father regularly, but he also made sure she would have a guard with her.

"I can't believe you did that," Dawn said, climbing into the car. "Why did you say anything?"

"Baby, I saw the glee in her eyes. She was going to hurt you whenever you were around her. I wasn't going to let that happen." He pulled away from the pack, happy that Francie was not going to get the chance to hurt anyone else.

"I can't believe Daddy did that," she said. "I thought he loved her."

"No, he didn't. She was a convenience for him, nothing more." Daniel drove back home.

Once inside the grounds, he felt the love of his pack surround him. Glancing at Dawn, he smiled. "Do you feel it?"

"Yes, I feel them. They're all happy for us. There's no jealousy. This is the way a pack is supposed to work." She leaned her head against the car seat. "I love you, Daniel."

"Baby, words can't even begin to describe what I feel for you." He reached out to touch her cheek. "We're going to have an amazing life together."

"Do you promise?" she asked.

"I won't accept anything but amazing."

****

Jake knocked on the window of the car causing her to jump. She'd been so taken by Daniel she hadn't heard anyone approach.

"What's the matter?" Daniel asked, opening his car door.

"I've got a mated couple in your sitting room. She was abused during her transition and was unable to feel pain. You wanted someone for Dawn to talk to, and I've found her." Jake tapped the hood of the car. "Come on, they're waiting to talk to you."

Intrigued, Dawn climbed out of the car and followed Daniel inside the house. She was about to meet someone who couldn't feel any pain. After what her father did to her mother, she didn't know if she was ready for anymore revelations.

Her mate wouldn't let her back out, and before she knew it they were in the sitting room being introduced to a beautiful blonde woman and her mate.

"Hi, I'm Lola, and this is my mate, Ben." The blonde made the introductions, giving them both a smile.

Dawn noticed Lola didn't spend too long noticing Daniel. She didn't like the thought of dealing with jealousy.

"It's great to meet you, Lola."

"Thanks. When Jake put the word out about wolves who couldn't feel pain, I knew I had to respond."

Taking a seat, Dawn crossed her legs and stared at Lola. "You can't feel pain. Please, have a seat." She waved her hands for them to take a seat opposite them. Daniel placed his hand along the back of the sofa, comforting her with his warmth.

"I wasn't very lucky with my parents. My father was a mean drunk, and my mother didn't care. I was hurt regularly growing up." Ben moved in close to rub his nose against Lola's cheek. "During my transition I was beaten because I couldn't leave the house to get food or alcohol for my father. It was the worst time of my life." Lola rubbed her hands down her thighs. "When it was all over everything returned to normal, but I noticed something was wrong about three days afterward. I got my dad the wrong brand of cigarettes, and he started to, erm, to hurt me. I couldn't feel anything. The pain, it wasn't registering. It has been over fifteen years since my transition."

"What did you do?" Dawn asked.

"I ran away from home. Dad started to notice that I wouldn't scream when he broke something. I couldn't feel anything. I was closed off, trapped, and there was nothing I could do to stop those feelings. I heard him arranging a fight for me to star in. A bloody battle to the death. I knew my time was going to be short lived. I took the savings I'd gotten and left." Lola chuckled, tears filling her eyes as she spoke. "I ended up on the streets because I didn't have enough money. Before I knew what was happening, I'd entered myself into the illegal fights. I fought fellow wolves or humans. I've killed a lot of people, and it was during a bad battle that I met Ben."

She smiled at Ben.

"I'm an alpha, and I intended to put an end to it. The moment I saw Lola I knew she was my mate. I also knew there was something different about her," Ben said.

"He took me home, and within a week we were mated. We couldn't control the mating bond." Lola stroked his face. "Afterward, I noticed I could feel pain." Lola turned to look at Dawn. "If I go without sharing blood for any length of time then I my ability to feel pain stops. It all depends on my bond with Ben." Lola touched her mate. The love between the two was pure, heart-warming.

"Has anything been different between you two? What about kids?" Daniel asked.

Ben's grin turned wicked. "We've got four kids back home. Her condition came in handy during the labor. Once you're with her during the first pregnancy, you'll see what I mean. I won't share blood with her for two months before giving birth. I couldn't stand to see her in pain."

"He's a real softy inside. Ben won't let anything happen to me." Lola turned back to look at them. "My condition is not a problem, and it won't be for you either. You're true mates, and he'll keep you safe."

Dawn looked at Daniel, the love of her life. "Thank you."

Lola and Ben stayed for dinner, but they needed to get back in order to keep their kids under some kind of control.

"They run rings around the pack taking care of

them."

Dawn stood beside Daniel as they waved goodbye. "What are you thinking?" she asked.

"I can't wait to see you swollen with my child." His hands went around her neck, securing a collar. "Dawn, would you do me the honor of becoming my wife and sub?"

Reaching up, she touched the small piece of jewelry.

Turning into his arms, she held him tightly, smiling. "Nothing would give me greater pleasure." She rubbed her nose against his, chuckling as she did.

Daniel picked her up, but instead of leading her into the house, he started to walk toward the cabin.

"What do you have on your mind, Sir?" she asked. Heat filled her core, spilling from the lips of her pussy.

"You know what I'm thinking. It's time I punished my little pet before she thinks she can top from the bottom."

He placed her on her feet and turned the light on. Peace and happiness settled over her. Going to her knees, Dawn was ready to become his submissive in all true senses of the word.

Epilogue

Two years later

Dawn sat on the lawn, sucking on a lollipop as Daniel started to bark out orders to the pack. A delivery of nursery equipment was coming today, and he wanted plenty of men on hand to help build it up. There was over seven months until she gave birth, but he was preparing early. She rubbed her slight bump, chuckling.

"You're going to be one loved kid," she said.

In the past two years her life had changed so dramatically. Her mother had been sentenced to the hunt. No one, not even Dawn, knew the true extent of her torture. She'd hurt many of the pack women on a regular basis, but they had been too afraid to go to Don. Since then, her father has been paying more attention to the people rather than the running of the pack to avoid wars.

She visited him often but only with a guard.

Touching the collar around her neck, she couldn't help but smile. Daniel was the perfect Dom, caring, and loving. She loved being his mate, and since their mating, she'd been able to feel.

She learned the hard way not to swallow steaming coffee. Now, at breakfast, Daniel wouldn't give her straight from the pot coffee. He helped her constantly to grow accustomed to actually feeling pain.

"What are you laughing at, pet?" he asked, sitting beside her.

Taking a slice of apple from the picnic basket, she moved between his thighs. "You and your need to have everything perfect." She moaned as he started to rub her shoulders. "That feels good."

He kissed her neck. "There'll be more where that came from." Daniel pressed a hand to her stomach. "I'm going to make sure you're taken care of, Dawn. If that means being prepared for the worst, then so be it."

"You've got three pack females training to be midwives. They've got more important things to do. I'm not giving birth here. I'm going to the nearest hospital to bring this little guy into the world."

"What makes you think it's a boy?" he asked.

"A feeling." She leaned back and smiled up at him. "His Daddy needs him to train."

He chuckled. "I don't care what we have so long as you're here for the growing up."

She kissed his lips as the truck arrived bringing the furniture. "I'll leave you to do your man thing."

"Your ass is so getting a spanking." Daniel left her on the lawn to go and organize their nursery.

Staring up into the sunlight, Dawn couldn't complain about life. She'd gone from feeling ashamed and scared, to embracing every little detail thrown her way.

Later that night, Daniel had showed her who was in charge of their relationship. He strapped her to the bed and spanked her ass until she was screaming for his cock. It didn't matter how much she begged, Daniel would only stop when he was good and ready.

Seven months later, Dawn didn't get her wish of going to the hospital. Little Brady came into the world, screaming, like his mother. She'd decided she wanted to feel every little second of pain of his birth. Daniel held her hand throughout it all. Once Brady was in her arms, the pain was worth it.

However, for the second child, Dawn settled on feeling no pain during her daughter's birth, and Daniel was more than happy with that.

The End

EVERNIGHT PUBLISHING ®

www.evernightpublishing.com

CPSIA information can be obtained
at www.ICGtesting.com
Printed in the USA
LVHW042139011222
734449LV00027B/376